KT-483-326

SUMMER OF LOVE

It's the summer of 1969: an exciting time of music and fashion, peace and love. However, the Swinging Sixties seem to have by-passed the village of Ashcote. There, 17-year-old Clemmie is thinking only of sitting her A-levels, gaining a place at university and the long, hot summer stretching ahead of her. But when she meets the gorgeous Lewis Coleman-Beck, Clemmie's life changes in a split-second and she is plunged, head-over-heels, into her very own Summer of Love.

London Borough of Lambeth	
0431966 4	
ᘰhᘰ	28·4·06
F	£8·99

CHRISTINA JONES

SUMMER OF LOVE

Complete and Unabridged

LINFORD
Leicester

First published in Great Britain in 2004

First Linford Edition
published 2006

Copyright © 2004 by Christina Jones
All rights reserved

British Library CIP Data

Jones, Christina, *1948* –
    Summer of love.—
    Large print ed.—
    Linford romance library
    1. Love stories
    2. Large type books
    I. Title
    823.9'14 [F]

ISBN 1–84617–301–9

Published by
F. A. Thorpe (Publishing)
Anstey, Leicestershire

Set by Words & Graphics Ltd.
Anstey, Leicestershire
Printed and bound in Great Britain by
T. J. International Ltd., Padstow, Cornwall

This book is printed on acid-free paper

1

It's as hot and drowsy as a July morning: impossible to believe that it's already September and we're closer to Christmas than midsummer. The flowers are still blowsy and vibrant; the air is sleepy, sultry, heavy with pollen and sweetness. Everyone says it's going to be a glorious autumn this year. A perfect Indian summer. Maybe it'll be like that other perfect summer so long ago when I was young . . .

Not that I'm ancient, of course. Well, I'm fifty-one now which is ancient by some standards — where on earth did the time go? — but that summer is still as vivid as if it were yesterday. I remember every detail, especially . . . but no, I really shouldn't think about that now. Not today of all days. After all, my present life is perfect: there's no need to look back to the past, is there?

I'm lounging indolently on the hammock swing in the garden with the Sunday papers, and I'm blissfully happy; totally contented with my life, and I know I'm lucky. But even so, being fifty-one has come as something of a shock. Can I *really* be fifty-one?

I smile to myself. Reaching fifty last year was fine: everyone said fifty was the new forty, and Lulu and Olivia Newton John and people like that were publicly proud to be fifty. But 'being in my fifties' sounds suspiciously like getting old to me, especially when inside my head I'm seventeen. Always seventeen.

Outwardly? Well, I've never been vain, but I do take care of myself. I'm a sucker for every anti-ageing cream on the market, and I dance myself silly by way of exercise and I still wear my faded jeans and an armful of silver bangles and walk barefoot on the grass. My hair is cut in trendy choppy layers — and if the addition of blonde highlights hide the first grey streaks, then it remains a secret between me and Pauline at Marcelle's Hair Salon.

Oh yes, if I close my eyes on this glorious morning and let the warmth wash over me, I can easily forget that I'm fifty-one years old. Removed from reality by the soporific silence of a Sunday morning, the people and places from the past seem far more real than those who live in my life now. Strange then, how those images from years ago seem to insist on marching through my head today . . .

I quickly open my eyes again and squint through the spiralling sun across the garden at my parents having coffee beneath the brightly striped umbrella. They'd be so disappointed if they knew where my thoughts are straying. They smile across at me, pleased that I'm here, looking forward to us all going out to lunch later. They're in their mid-seventies now, still very happy together, but I wonder if they ever really forgave me.

I know they said they did, and after

all, it's a lifetime ago, but at the time . . .

Why on earth does my mind insist on going down that route? What is it about today, of all days, that makes me want to recall the past? I really mustn't dwell on it. But I could so easily give into the temptation, and remember.

Maybe it's not only because of the weather, but also because I'm here in my parents' neat, orderly semi? The house where I grew up, the house in Ashcote, the sprawling Berkshire village that was my childhood home. The house where I broke their hearts.

I still feel real pangs of guilt at their remembered anger and grief, which is confusing as most of my memories of that time are happy ones. I know I shouldn't be self-indulgent and allow myself to reminisce, but the seductive scents of the warm earth and the flowers and the sleepy rhythmic murmur of the bees could belong so easily to that other summer more than thirty years ago.

The summer that I really shouldn't keep going back to. My forbidden summer. The summer that changed my life.

2

1969 had to be the best time in the whole history of the world to be seventeen, I decided. There were so many amazing changes taking place, all adding vibrant colour and a buzz of excitement to the end of my growing-up decade, and I loved being young and alive and happy.

I was captivated by the hippie peace and freedom movement, and avidly watched the eccentrically dressed teenagers on television as they bravely protested about everything from the Vietnam War to racial equality. And then there was the advent of the mind-blowing psychedelic music with rock bands, groups of gorgeous and glamorous boys, stirring up frenzies of adolescent lust in dance halls across the country.

Not, of course, that any of this had

made much impact on Ashcote. Ashcote, still rooted somewhere pre-war, had never been quite ready for the Sixties. The nearest we'd ever got to a rock band was the Ezra Samuels Caribbean Trio playing in the village hall on party nights. With a network of high-banked and tree-shrouded lanes feeding away from either side of the High Street, Ashcote was typical of many large Berkshire villages, having its origins in agriculture and accepting the creeping of commerce with a seemingly sulky reluctance. The High Street, which housed the brand new all-girls' grammar school at one end and a garage at the other, had various shops, the village hall, a pub — which I'd been forbidden to even think about visiting — in between.

It was midday. Early June. 1969. I'd just had lunch with my Mum in the garden, and was heading for school with several classmates, all of us knowing that in less than half an hour we'd have to forget all about hippies and rock bands, the sunshine and the flowers and the summer sounds of Tony Blackburn on Radio One, and listen to those dreaded words: 'You may turn your papers over now . . .'

Only four more exams to go. One English paper this afternoon, then two Religious Education and the last History of Art. Then the agonising wait for the results of course, and then in the autumn, with my requisite number of graded passes, off to university.

University was a scarily thrilling prospect. I'd never been away from home alone before. In fact, apart from occasional holidays when my parents could afford them, I'd rarely left the village.

An only child, my parents were inordinately proud of my achievements. No-one else on either side of the family had ever been to university or even stayed on at school. Mum and Dad had been ecstatic when I'd passed my 11+, and even more so — if that were possible — when I'd passed all 9 O levels with good grades. They expected me to sail through the As — and told simply everyone who would listen about me going to university.

I'd had my interviews at Durham — an excursion of such mammoth proportions that I felt I might as well have been emigrating to Australia — and they'd offered a provisional place to read English as long as I gained a minimum of an A in English and two Bs. All the way home on the train, Mum had been loudly and embarrassingly confident that I'd manage those grades because I enjoyed the subjects, liked learning, worked hard, loved school, didn't I? I was a model pupil and they were so proud of me.

Mum and Dad had always taken the time to explain things to me, to answer my questions. They'd always talked to me, we'd always discussed everything, and they'd instilled the joy of learning about new things, and the importance of treasuring the old, in me from an early age.

If I succeeded it was simply because of them, I owed them everything and I knew I'd never let them down.

Anyway, once the A levels were over there were weeks and weeks of lazy enjoyment to look forward to before the learning started all over again, although I'd probably have to take a holiday job. Mum and Dad were going to find it difficult to get all the things I needed for university even with the grant. But I'd plan for after-the-exams later. Today I had to think about Dickens and Chaucer and Shakespeare and Joseph Conrad and Stella Gibbons.

Actually, the English Literature exam held no terrors at all — I was saving my terror for the RE ones looming next week because RE was my weakest subject of the three — I loved reading, was delighted by the English set books, and revising had seemed like pure pleasure rather than hard work.

I drifted along the sun-baked lane between the head-high columbine and dog roses; with the sky stretching cloudless above me and the ground white-hot in the glare of the sun. Dawn and Jenny were on either side of me, and we were singing a silly song we'd made up to the tune of The Hollies' *Sorry Suzanne*. It was supposed to help us remember the plot of Othello, but actually I didn't need any help at all. I thought that the story was so wonderfully heartbreaking. All that love, all that jealousy . . .

I wondered if anyone would ever love me enough to want me dead rather than see me in the arms of another man. As I'd never had a proper boyfriend, it was all rather academic, but the passionate tragedy of Desdemona and Iago and Othello filled my dreams.

'Clemmie!'

I stopped walking. Dawn and Jenny went on, still singing, arms linked.

I grinned at Paula Conway who was sitting on the wall outside the Ashcote Stores. 'You look very glamorous.'

'You don't,' Paula laughed, pointing

11

at my hated straw boater. We had to wear them — on pain of death — all the time we were in uniform. 'Mind you, if you yank that dress up any higher the whole of Ashcote will be able to see your knickers.'

I looked down at my even more hated blue and while striped shirtwaister, which, like all the Sixth Form, I'd bundled over and over the top of my navy blue elasticated money belt.

'Only another couple of weeks then this lot'll be chucked in the bin for ever — look, sorry Paula, but I really can't stop, I've got English this afternoon. Wish me luck.'

'You won't need any luck, Clem. You're clever enough to pass your A levels with one hand tied behind your back, and with your eyes closed, and having done no revision at all — unlike me.'

I laughed. Paula lived three doors away from me and had escaped from the Secondary Modern as soon as it was legally possible with no qualifications in anything at all. We'd grown up together, and were still friends; although now she worked in the trendiest record shop in Reading and had a new boyfriend every weekend, she seemed years older than I was rather than simply a few months.

'Why aren't you at work?'

'Half-day closing. I caught the early bus home. I usually stay in town and do some shopping, but I'm — um — seeing someone this afternoon.'

I groaned in sheer envy at the grown-upness of it all. Staying in town to do shopping . . . The luxury of a half-day off . . . Seeing a mysterious someone . . .

'I wish I was you.'

'No, you don't,' Paula slid from the wall and swung herself round, her glossy bobbed Cilla Black hair and her pink swirly mini dress, moving in one fluid motion. 'You'd be bored to tears with my life. When you've passed your exams and been to university you'll be able to do whatever you like. You'll get a proper job and earn loads of money and have a fast car and a lovely house and — '

'I'd settle for having some money right now.'

Paula stopped grinning. 'Yeah, it must be a drag trying to live on pocket money. Look, if you're serious, Clemmie, one of our Saturday girls left last week. Shall I ask if they've replaced her yet, and if not, I'll put your name forward, shall I?'

'Yes, please!' I still looked enviously at her clothes and her hairdo. I knew I'd have to put some money away, but surely I'd be able to spend a bit on myself? 'That'd be wonderful. And once the exams are over I can work all week, not just Saturdays, if they need anyone — until I go to university of course.'

'Oh, of course.' Paula pulled a teasing face. 'Okay, I'll ask tomorrow and let you know. Now it looks as if your friends want you, so you'd better run along like a good little schoolgirl.'

'Okay, okay,' I flapped my hands towards Dawn and Jenny who were motioning me to hurry up. 'Paula — I'll see you later — and thanks.'

'You're welcome. And good luck with the exam. Not that you'll need it, of course.'

'Thanks — and good luck with whoever you're meeting. Not that you'll need any luck there, either.'

I could still hear her chuckling as I caught up with Jenny and Dawn.

'I don't know why you're still friends with her,' Dawn said as we hurried towards the school gates. 'She's got a heck of a reputation.'

'She's a bit of a — well, you know . . . ' Jenny giggled. 'And you'll get tarred with the same brush, Clem, if you hang around with her.'

'I don't hang around with her,' I said crossly. 'Though sometimes I wish I did. She has a great life. Working in Sheldon Busby's and being able to buy records and clothes and make-up and have boyfriends and — '

'And that's exactly what she'll still be doing in twenty years time,' Dawn said.

'Working in a record shop. And she'll probably have half a dozen kids and will never have moved away from Ashcote.'

'Whereas we,' Jenny said, 'will have the world at our feet.'

Giggling even more at the thought of the world bowing to three teenagers from Ashcote, we pushed our way out of the blazing sun and into the cool darkness of the school. It was only two years old and still smelled new: three storeys, all trendy grey concrete and chrome, big windows, the spiral staircases visible, the girls teeming up and down inside like so many ants. We'd moved there from the old Grammar School fifteen miles away and it was great to be able to walk to school and go home for lunch; and for the well-stocked modern labs and art rooms and domestic science rooms, to be pristine and gleaming.

Snatching off our hats as we lined up with the rest of the afternoon's A levellers, I decided not to tell Jenny and Dawn that Paula might get me a holiday job working with her at Sheldon Busby's. Somehow I had the feeling they wouldn't approve.

'Hurry up, girls!' Miss Edwards, our English teacher, was standing outside the assembly hall. 'Stop chattering! You've got fifteen minutes before the exam starts. And leave your things here. They should be in your lockers — you know you've been told not to bring those talisman toys into school. Fluffy teddies at your age — really! Pencil cases and your brains are the only things you'll need in the exam room! I trust you've all got both?'

'Yes, Miss Edwards,' we all chorused diligently, as we trooped into the hall to meet our fate.

3

Emerging three hours later, exhausted but delighted that the essay questions had been exactly what I would have chosen, I couldn't wait to get home and tear off my school uniform and sit in the back garden under the cherry trees listening to the radio. No more exams now for a week. I'd start my RE revision tomorrow, but today, I was free!

Dawn and Jenny were equally happy with the exam, so we strolled along Ashcote's sleepy lanes, singing Donovan's *Colours*, pretty sure that we were one step closer to academic stardom.

Mum made a huge fuss of me when I got home, serving up a high tea of tinned salmon and salad in the garden by way of celebration. I'd scrambled out of my uniform and pulled on my jeans and T-shirt, and let my hair slide out of its regulation ponytail, and now, with my ever-present transistor radio, was sitting on the grass in the still-hot sun, listening to *Make It Easy On Yourself* by the Walker Brothers. It was absolutely my most favourite song ever. The words never failed to make my heart break — and Scott Walker's deep, sensual voice sent butterflies looping the loop in my stomach.

This was probably why I didn't hear Paula scrunch along the gravelled path, click through our front gate, or call her usual cheery 'hiya' to Mum in the kitchen as she passed.

'How did it go then?' She plonked herself down beside me, carefully pulling her ridiculously short dress decorously down to the tops of her thighs.

The Walker Brothers had been replaced by the Beach Boys on the radio. I turned down the volume. 'Fine, thanks. What about you and your mystery man?'

'Fantastic,' Paula smirked.

'Is this a new boyfriend then? Do I know him? God, it's not Nick, is it?'

Nick Rayner was Ashcote's heart-throb. Dawn and Jenny and I had his name written all over our pencil cases and our folders and books and even engraved on the inside of our desk lids. He was two years older than us and had a motorbike and was what our parents called 'undesirable' — although we of course thought he was the most desirable thing in the entire universe.

'No!' Paula laughed. 'I dumped Nick ages ago. He's just a boy. This one is a real man.'

'*What?*' I wrinkled my nose. I didn't even know that Paula had been out with Nick Rayner. Dawn and Jenny would be spitting venom. They'd actually cried when Paul McCartney had married Linda a few months before, so this news would really upset them. I concentrated on not looking jealous. 'So how old is he then, this — er — man? Really, really old?'

'About twenty one,' Paula said

proudly. 'And he's got a Ford Capri.'

I sat in admiring silence. Twenty-one was seriously grown-up. And the Ford Capri was the newest, sportiest, hottest car on the market this year. No-one I knew had ever had a boyfriend with a car — let alone something as swish and expensive as that.

'Where did you meet him?'

'At work. He came into the shop to listen to some records and I served him and our eyes met and . . . ' Paula's face was far-away-dreamy. 'He's dead lovely — you know, all lean and fit, and he's got fab long silky hair, and when he speaks he makes my knees turn to jelly. He's educated, Clem. Not like the oiks round here. He's got a dead posh voice and he uses lovely words.'

I wanted to laugh. 'He sounds like someone straight out of a magazine love story! Are you sure you haven't made him up?'

Paula, who had probably never read a whole book in her life, was always reading the picture stories in teenage magazines, and I'd always teased her that she believed they were real.

'No, of course I haven't made him up!' Paula glared at me. 'I don't need to live in a land of make-believe — unlike some people, I do have real boyfriends.'

I winced. 'Okay — so what's his name?'

'That's for me to know and you to find out.'

I giggled. 'Bet he's called Algernon, then. And where does he live?'

'Er — well, he's not from round here. Although I think he's living near here at the moment, which is why he came into the shop.' She rolled on to her stomach and ran her fingers with their pearly pink nails, through the grass. 'He is out of this world.'

For a fleeting moment I wondered jealously why this mysterious, gorgeous someone, who, if Paula was to be believed, was clearly rich and old and educated and handsome, would be interested in her? Surely, if he was that dishy he'd be able to have his pick of all the girls? Why would he settle for someone like Paula, who wasn't very bright and looked, well — tarty?

Mind you, I knew all about Paula's reputation in the village for being 'anyone's' as my Mum said, so maybe that was the attraction.

Still, it seemed to me that for all her boasting, Paula didn't know much about this man at all. Maybe she had made him up. Maybe she'd made it up about going out with Nick Rayner, too. I really, really hoped so.

'When will we get to see him, then?'

Paula looked up at me, her false eyelashes casting deep dark crescent shadows on her cheeks. 'If you get the job in Sheldon Busby's you'll definitely see him — he's in all the time. Can't keep away from me.'

I laughed wistfully. I wished I could say that about someone. Especially Nick Rayner. 'So why were you meeting him this afternoon and not tonight, then?'

'God, you ask so many questions,

Clemmie!' Paula studied her finger-nails. 'He's — um — well, he says he's busy in the evenings. He probably works shifts or something.'

I nodded. That might be true. My Dad, as a coach driver, was rarely at home when other people were. But even so . . . 'And maybe he's married.'

'Of course he isn't married! I do have some principles, you know! Anyway,' Paula scrambled quickly to her feet, 'I only came round to say I haven't forgotten about the Saturday job, oh, and to see how your exam went, of course.'

'No you didn't,' I grinned at her. 'You came round to brag about Mr Wonderful!'

Mum appeared from the kitchen at that moment, carrying a tray with glasses of home-made ginger beer. She smiled at Paula. 'I didn't know you were here, dear. I didn't hear you come round. I'll get another glass.'

'No thanks, Mrs Long. I'm not stopping. 'Bye, Clemmie — I'll see you tomorrow.'

We both watched her shimmy out of the gate.

'She gets worse,' Mum said with deep disapproval. 'All that make-up — and that dress — she might as well not be wearing anything. What did she want, anyway?'

I decided not to mention Mr Wonderful. Mum would go on about it for hours.

'She's going to see if she can get me a Saturday job in Sheldon Busby's — so I can save some money for university,' I added quickly. 'Then, once the exams are over, I can work there through the holidays too. I know I'll get a grant, but it'll be handy to have some extra money, won't it? I know how hard you and Dad have been saving and I'd like to add some too.'

'Oh, right,' Mum seemed to be searching for some argument to this suggestion, but couldn't find one. 'Well, as long as that's all it is — I wouldn't want you to get too friendly with her — that is, I know you're friends, but I wouldn't like to think you and she . . . well, you know what I mean?'

'Yes, Mum.' I reached for the ginger beer trying not to laugh.

Paula's parents both worked full time in Reading, so she had the house to herself most of the time, and had done since she was a little girl. Her Mum would never be there when she and all her brothers and sisters came home from school, and never cooked proper meals, they seemed to live out of the fish and chip shop, and she'd certainly never, ever make ginger beer . . .

My Mum worked as a cleaner at Ashcote Mixed Infants a few minutes along the lane, so she was always around for me. Sometimes, treacherously, I wished I could be a bit more independent. Oh, it was lovely coming home from school and knowing Mum was there and that there'd be a hot meal on the table and I'd never have to worry about being on my own — but I was seventeen now. I didn't need looking after.

'Anyway,' Mum said, 'if it's a bit of extra cash you're after, they're still needing pickers up at Honeydew for their first crop. I know you won't be able to do much until the exams are over, but it'll be a help. I'm thinking of going up there myself.'

I sipped my ginger beer. Honeydew Farm, on the outskirts of the village, was known across the county for its fruit. The orchards stretched for miles, and in summer the strawberry fields were filled with casual pickers from Ashcote and the surrounding area.

'I could do that as well,' I said eagerly. 'I could cycle up there in the morning and do a few hours. Strawberry picking pays really well and I haven't got another exam for a week. I won't need to revise all the time.'

'Are you sure? RE isn't your strongest subject, is it? Wouldn't it be better to wait until afterwards?'

I shook my head, dreaming of having clothes like Paula's, and being able to get my long schoolgirly hair cut in a proper style, and buy a pair or three of false eyelashes, and then Nick Rayner might really notice me.

'I think it'd do me good to do something that's not involved with studying and school. And I could take my books and mug up while I'm picking. And I'd be out in the fresh air. And it won't be all day every day. Oh, go on, Mum — it's a great idea. And after all, you suggested it.'

'I should have kept my mouth shut,' Mum smiled, knowing I'd get my own way. 'All right, but if it starts to interfere with your studying you're to give it up. Promise me?'

'I promise.'

4

The next morning, as the sun was spiralling gauzily through the rows of truncated apple, plum and cherry trees with their froth of blossoms, and a heat haze hovered over the miles of strawberry fields, I leaned my bicycle against one of Honeydew's litchen-covered red brick barns, and joined the queue at the door.

I'd been strawberry picking with Mum — and sometimes Dad when his shifts allowed — at Honeydew since I was a little girl. I knew everyone in the queue, and Mr Leach, the estate manager who was doing the weighing and paying, knew me.

'Hello, young Clemmie.' He wrote my name in the ledger and gave me a teasing look. 'I didn't think we'd get you along here this year. Thought you'd be too grand for us — what with you going up to the varsity and all — or at least, that's what your Dad tells everyone in the pub. Have you had enough of all that book-learning and decided to become a farm labourer?'

'I'm saving up for when I go away,' I took my towering pile of punnets and patted my beaded shoulder bag. 'And I've got my books in here for studying at lunch time, so if Mum and Dad ask you — '

'I'll tell 'em you've been working like a Trojan on all accounts,' he winked at me. 'Don't you eat too many strawberries and make yourself ill, mind, or your Dad'll have my guts for garters. Right, who's next?'

Balancing my pile of punnets under my chin, I set off to the far side of the field. It meant a longer walk back once the punnets were filled, but also meant that the biggest, juiciest strawberries were still untouched. And the biggest, juiciest strawberries weighed the most and therefore filled the punnets more quickly and earned more money.

I squatted down between the rows, the tiny mounds of straw snaking away as far as the eye could see, the green leaves and glistening red first crop strawberries sitting proudly atop them. It was already hot, and the drowsy air was still and almost silent. I couldn't hear anything except the distant voices on the other side of the field, and the birdsong and the occasional faraway vroom of a car on the Reading road.

With the sun on my back, warming me through my jeans and skimpy T-shirt, I picked steadily for a while, careful to snap the hulls just below the rosette of leaves with my thumbnails, not bruising the fruit. I knew only too well that Mr Leach's eagle eyes never missed bruised fruit and he'd chuck it into the jam bucket and I wouldn't get paid.

The punnets filled quickly, and I sat back on the baked ground, easing my knees and shoulders. Popping yet another strawberry into my mouth, I wondered if I should have a quick skim through my RE notes. I took my revision folder reluctantly from my bag. It wasn't an appealing prospect. I wished we'd been studying the New Testament, which was far more familiar, not to mention relevant and interesting, rather than the Old Testament Prophets. They were such a miserable bunch.

'Excuse me . . . '

I squinted up against the vivid blueness of the sky and the dazzle of the sun.

A tall figure loomed over me. I knew it was young and male, but couldn't make out his features. For a wonderful moment I thought it might be Nick Rayner — but then Nick would never have said excuse me.

'Yes?'

'I found this on the path back there. Is it yours? Did you drop it?'

He came closer and handed me my RE text book. Like Nick Rayner, he was tall and slim and dark. Like Nick Rayner, he wore tight faded jeans and a black T-shirt. But that's where the similarity ended. Not even Nick looked remotely like a cross between David Bowie and Scott Walker. Not even Nick could compare to this: simply the most beautiful boy in the world.

'Oh, thank you,' I mumbled, totally flustered. 'Yes, it must have dropped out of my bag. That's really kind of you . . . um . . . I mean, thank you.'

'You're welcome,' he straightened up, pushing his silky hair from his eyes, and smiled at me.

And that was it. Honestly. I fell in love. Head over heels. At first sight.

'Er — are you strawberry picking, too?' I immediately knew it was a stupid question. He didn't have any punnets and he simply didn't look like a picker. I also knew I was blushing redder than any of the strawberries. 'That is — '

He shook his head. 'I'm staying with my Godparents at Honeydew for a few weeks. I was just on my way out along the track there when I found your book. I'm Lewis Coleman-Beck — and I know you're Clemmie Long.'

My mouth dropped open. 'Blimey! I mean — '

'I'm not a mind-reader,' his voice was smooth and husky all at the same time, and hinted at laughter. 'It's written on the front of your book.'

I blushed even more. My name was on the book and so was 'Clemmie loves Nick Rayner for ever and ever' and millions of little hearts with arrows through them.

'Clemmie's an unusual name. Is it short for Clemency?'

'Clementine,' I muttered, wishing I was wearing glamorous clothes and that my blonde hair was in some sort of trendy style instead of tumbling wildly down my back, and that I had at least four pairs of false eyelashes on and didn't look like a gauche schoolgirl. 'After Winston Churchill's wife. My parents were huge admirers.'

'It's lovely,' Lewis Coleman-Beck nodded. 'And as I said, unusual. As is your reading matter. Jeremiah? Isaiah?

The gloom and doom prophets?'

'RE A levels. Next week.' My mouth was growing dryer by the minute. I prayed I didn't have strawberry juice on my chin.

He pulled a face. 'A levels — oh, dear. I remember them well. I flunked all mine the first time round. Not that it mattered too much. I passed the re-sits after months of awful cramming.'

'Mine matter a lot,' I said. 'I'm going to university.'

'I did that, too,' Lewis Coleman-Beck said ruefully. 'And dropped out after the first year. I was a massive disappointment to my parents. I'm sure you'll be far more successful. Anyway, I mustn't keep you from your studying or your strawberry picking. It was nice meeting you.'

'And you,' I said faintly, knowing that he was going to walk away from me. Knowing that he'd walk out of my life forever. Knowing it would break my heart if he did.

He started heading towards Honeydew's car park, then he stopped, turned and smiled again. 'I don't suppose you'd like to come out for a drink or something, sometime? I mean, I realise you're busy with exams, but I don't know many people round here and — '

'I'd love to,' I heard myself saying. There was no way on earth that I'd tell him I'd never been inside a public house in my life. That apart from sweet sherry at Christmas I'd never touched alcohol. That I wasn't even old enough to drink. 'That'd be really nice.'

'Shall I ring you?'

'We're not on the phone at home.' None of my friends were on the phone. Only the really well-off people in Ashcote were on the phone. No doubt Lewis Coleman-Beck would think this was very quaint.

'Oh, well, in that case we'd better make a date right now. How about tomorrow evening? Shall I come and collect you?'

I shook my head quickly. 'Collect' sounded as if he had a car. Mum and Dad would never in a million years let me go off with a strange man in a car. They'd never let me go off with a strange man full stop. My mind was whirling. 'Er — we could meet up here — at about seven? Outside the main gates?'

'Outside the gates at seven it is,' he smiled. 'See you tomorrow night, Clemmie.'

I nodded, watching him walk away. I knew then that if I met Lewis Coleman-Beck tomorrow my life would never be the same again. Was it a risk I was prepared to take?

5

'For goodness sake, hurry up,' Paula snapped at me. 'Mr Smithson hasn't got all day! He's agreed to see you in the lunch hour as a special favour to me.'

After a sleepless night in which I'd tossed and turned, one minute grinning into the darkness at the thought of going out with the gorgeous Lewis Coleman-Beck and the next shivering in misery because I knew he wouldn't turn up, and all the while knowing, for the first time in my life, that I was going to lie to my parents, I really wasn't ready for a job interview.

Paula had phoned Ashcote Mixed Infants that morning, spoken to my Mum, and I'd been told to catch the next bus into Reading for the interview with Sheldon Busby's manager. Paula said she'd meet me at the bus station, and give me a few tips before we reached the shop.

It was the last thing I'd wanted to do. I'd thought of nothing but Lewis from the moment we'd met twenty seven hours earlier. I wanted to spend all day preening and primping and trying to find something in my wardrobe that might just make Lewis think, when we met for the second time, that I was a grown up. As it was also the first time that I'd had a proper date — being walked home by the youth club boys who I'd known all my life didn't count — I was gibbering with nerves.

'Okay,' I snapped back at Paula as we hurtled towards The Butts through crowds of sweating shoppers. 'Stop nagging. I can't walk in these sandals.'

'You look like Dick Emery,' Paula laughed over her shoulder. 'Don't know why you bothered dressing up.'

As money was always short at home, my clothes, by necessity, were bought to last. I lived in jeans that were almost falling apart and things that came from jumble sales. Not that it mattered that much. With my long wild hair, the rag-bag look gave me a very up to the minute hippy-ish air. For the interview I'd selected a skirt that was too long and a top that was too big and borrowed Mum's best high-heeled sandals. I'd also tried to put my hair up, which was a huge mistake, as tendrils were now escaping everywhere at a rate of knots.

We came to a halt outside Sheldon Busby's and Paula looked sternly at me. 'Now, just be yourself. Don't try to be smart. Mr Smithson hates wafflers. If he asks, tell him you're honest, quick to learn, can handle money and add up. Tell him you're a good-time-keeper and that you know all about music.'

I nodded like an automaton. The sun scorched down between the tall grey buildings, and the tram lines glistened like molten silver, criss-crossing the junction. I was trembling — but it had nothing to do with the impending interview. For a fleeting moment I wondered if I should ask Paula for advice on my date with Lewis Coleman-Beck. What should I wear? What should I talk about? Where should I ask him to take me seeing as the village pub was completely out of the question?

I thought better of it. Paula was a real gossip, and if I wanted to keep my date with Lewis a secret, which I did, telling her would be like putting an announcement in the Ashcote Advertiser. No, if she could have her clandestine meetings with her older man with his Ford Capri and his mysterious evening occupation which was probably a wife and family, then I could keep my own counsel about Lewis. I'd find something to wear, and there wasn't much I could do about my hair anyway, and eyeliner, a few coats of mascara, and some lip gloss would probably be enough make-up as my face was reasonably tanned.

Paula gave me a little shove. 'Stop day-dreaming! Mr Smithson's not that scary — he's quite sweet, really. Come on!'

Outwardly, Sheldon Busby's hadn't changed much for a hundred years, having four huge display windows: one for musical instruments, one for records, one for sheet music, and the other filled with all the intricate bits and pieces vital to the professional musician. Taking a deep breath, I followed Paula through the set-back door of the records section.

The Beatles were belting out *Get Back* from an unseen amplifier, the lights were dimmed, it was stiflingly hot, and the walls were covered in signed posters and photographs of really famous rock stars. All down the middle of the shop there were rows of tiered stands filled with records: LPs, EPs, 45s, even some 78s, and a wide counter along two walls with several constantly-ringing cash registers and even more records stacked behind, beside and above it. People were three-deep round the displays, the two girls behind the counter were working flat-out, and it was unbelievably noisy.

I'd been here before, of course. Dawn

and Jenny and I often came to browse, or to ask Paula or whoever was serving, to play the record we liked most at the time so that we could go into the booths and listen over and over again. We rarely bought anything because we couldn't afford it. To work here, to be paid to work here, to get a staff discount off any record I liked, would be heaven . . .

'Paula! At last!' A plump, balding man appeared from behind the counter, his voice raised above Paul McCartney screaming at Jo-Jo to get back. 'And this must be your little friend.'

'Clemmie Long, yes.' Paula yelled back. 'I'll leave her with you. Linda and Jane look like they need a hand.'

She pushed her way behind the counter, leaving me and Mr Smithson facing one another. I very much hoped we weren't going to have the interview in the middle of the shop, bawling at each other like a pair of fishwives.

'Come into a booth!' Mr Smithson shouted. 'It's quieter in there!'

Thrusting through the crowded shop, I followed him into one of the glass-fronted listening booths, wobbling unsteadily on my Mum's sandals.

He closed the door, instantly shutting out the babble of the shop. The booths could comfortably hold four people, and had a sort of dark red perforated egg-box material cladding the ceiling, floor and walls to act as insulation. There were a couple of little bucket seats and speakers protruding above our heads. It was silent, claustrophobic and very, very warm: almost like being trapped under-water but without the water.

Mr Smithson was sweating even more than I was. He had damp patches all over his yellow nylon shirt, his face was beaded and even the top of his bald head glistened.

'Sorry about this but I don't have an office as such. As you can see, we're very busy. Saturdays are even worse. Paula says you're a clever girl and I'm short staffed. Ever worked in a shop before?'

'No, I haven't, but — '

'Not to worry. You'll soon learn. Handled money?'

'No, but then — '

'As long as it goes into the till and not into your pocket that's all I need to know!' Mr Smithson suddenly roared with laughter, the sound bouncing back at us both from the padded walls.

'Oh, I'm honest and — '

'Course you are,' Mr Smithson mopped his face with a damp hankie. 'And Paula says you're off to university which means you're as bright as a button. Start Saturday. Half past eight 'til half past five.'

'You mean — I've got the job?'

'Of course you've got the job,' Mr Smithson laughed again, dabbing at his upper lip.

'Er — thank you . . . Really? I mean . . . um — you want me to start *this* Saturday?'

'This Saturday or not at all, I'm afraid, my dear. I need someone as soon as possible, and if you can't start then,

then I'll have to advertise . . . '

I groaned inwardly. There were five days to go to the first RE exam, and I'd done no revision at all . . . Today was out because of getting ready to meet Lewis and now I'd be working on Saturday and — I shook my head. 'No, please — I'd love to take the job and this Saturday will be fine. Thank you so much . . . '

Mr Smithson beamed. 'Good-oh. We'll show you the ropes on Saturday, although I'm sure you'll soon pick everything up, a clever girl like you. Oh, goodness me, I nearly forgot the most important bit. Three pounds ten shillings do you to start?'

'Oh, yes. Yes. That'll be loads — I mean — yes, thank you . . . '

'Of course, we'll look at increasing it to four pounds later, if you're any good — now I must get back to my counter . . . ' He held out his hand. 'Welcome to Sheldon Busby's my dear.'

I shook his hand, which was very hot and slippery, in a total daze. Three pounds ten! I'd never had so much money in my entire life. I could put a thirty shillings a week away in my post office savings account for university and still afford to buy clothes and make-up and . . .

We shot out into the shop, and the noise and the heat swamped me from head to toe. The Who had taken over from The Beatles and were flooding Sheldon Busby's with the manic strains of *Pinball Wizard*. Paula grinned at me from behind the counter and gave me a thumbs up in triumph over the customers' heads. I beamed back and staggered out of the shop into Reading's scorchingly hot streets, hardly able to believe that it had been that easy.

As I travelled back to Ashcote on the bus, my head was still reeling from the events of the last twenty four hours: yesterday I was simply a schoolgirl bogged down by exams, today I'd not only got a job and money, but also, if he turned up of course, a boyfriend . . .

6

By half-past six, having not been able to eat any tea and having been quizzed relentlessly by Mum and Dad about whether I was ill or not, I'd hidden my bicycle behind one of Honeydew's sheds and was pacing up and down the lane outside the main gates.

I felt like a criminal. I'd rushed out of the house telling Mum and Dad that I was off to Jenny's to tell her about my success at Sheldon Busby's and to do my RE revision. I'd never been untruthful before. I'd never needed to be. But I knew they wouldn't let me go out with Lewis Coleman-Beck. Even if they had approved, they'd have wanted to meet him first, and quiz him about his family, and they'd have wanted to know where we were going and what time we'd be back. And they'd definitely think he was far too old for me

— and anyway they certainly wouldn't let me go out with anyone at all until the A levels were over.

It had been awful enough as it was. Both Mum and Dad had been pleased that I'd got the job at Sheldon Busby's but had voiced real concern over how much it was going to interfere with my exams.

'Surely you could wait a couple of weeks, love?' Dad had said, mopping up his gravy with a slice of bread. 'You've got your strawberry picking money for the time being — and working all day in a shop is going to make you very tired. Wouldn't it be wiser to wait until the exams are over?'

I'd explained that Mr Smithson wouldn't hold the job open and that I'd make sure I did extra revision to make up for Saturday, which was why I was going to Jenny's so that we could test each other. Then Mum had asked why I'd had a bath and washed my hair in the middle of the afternoon; why I was wearing so much make-up; and why had I dressed up in my best jeans and my silver flip-flops and the black chiffon shirt with the silver stars that tied at the waist, just to go to Jenny's.

I'd blushed and muttered about being really, really hot and dirty when I got back from Reading and needing to freshen up, and the make-up — heavy black eyeliner, loads of mascara and the palest shimmery beige lipstick — was some that Paula had lent me which I was trying out because I'd need to wear it for work. It was almost unbearable when they'd both smiled fondly and believed me.

Honeydew's fields were still filled with fruit pickers; it was a hot, motionless evening, with the sun brazen in a dark blue sky. As I skulked in the shadows of the hawthorn hedge in case anyone saw me and reported straight back to Mum and Dad, I felt more sick than I'd ever felt in my life.

Lewis Coleman-Beck simply wasn't going to turn up. I knew he wasn't. And if he did — what were we going to do?

What on earth would we have in common? What would we talk about? What if he wanted to kiss me? It was an awful admission, but at seventeen I'd never kissed a boy — not properly — before. The pursed-lipped pecks and near-misses during youth club games of Postman's Knock certainly hadn't given me the sort of experience someone like Lewis Coleman-Beck would expect . . .

'Pull yourself together,' I muttered under my breath. 'Don't let him know how naïve you are. Act all cool and sophisticated. Like Paula.'

The clock on the village church chimed seven in the distance. That was it. He wasn't coming. All my bravado melted away and I wanted to cry. I turned to grab my bike and go home before anyone saw my tears or witnessed my humiliation at being stood up.

'Clemmie, hi. Oh, you look lovely. Sorry if I've kept you — have you been waiting long?'

Lewis was pulling open Honeydew's

big wrought iron gates, smiling at me. His jeans were still faded and his T-shirt was white. His dark hair fell glossily towards his eyes. I looked at him and my heart did a sort of back-flip and my legs wobbled alarmingly. I tried to speak but my tongue had glued itself to the roof of my mouth.

I swallowed. 'Er — oh, no . . . not at all . . . I've just got here . . . '

He grinned at me. 'You should have come up to the house if you didn't want me to meet you at yours. I realised that earlier — it was very rude of me not to suggest it. There was no need to wait out here. Jess and Henry would have been only too pleased to meet you.'

I smiled weakly. Jess and Henry — his Godparents — Mr and Mrs Hawton-Ledley who were regarded in Ashcote as the lord and lady of the manor, who more or less owned the village, who held summer fetes and Christmas parties as token gestures to the hoi-polloi, who bestowed their favours on the peasants like passing royalty. Oh yes, they'd have welcomed me with open arms!

I smiled again, not knowing what to say to him. It had been so easy to chat yesterday morning — tonight was a different matter entirely when I was nervous and gauche and totally tongue-tied.

He walked across to me and kissed my cheek. He smelled faintly of sunshine and clean skin and lemon shampoo. 'You really do look fantastic. That's a fabulous shirt. It really suits you. With your beautiful hair you look like a real hippie star child.'

I still said nothing. Was I supposed to graciously accept the compliment or tell the truth about the shirt's Oxfam origins? To be honest, I could do neither coherently because I was trembling from head to toe simply because he'd brushed his lips against my face. I just gave what I hoped was a cheerful grin of thanks, although my lips didn't seem to move much.

'I do have a bit of a confession to

make,' he held out his hand. 'I hope you'll forgive me, but you weren't really looking forward to going for a drink, were you?'

I ignored his hand. I knew that if I held his hand he'd feel me trembling and *know*.

I managed to find something that resembled my voice. 'No, of course not. I don't mind not going to the pub at all.' If only he knew just *how* relieved I was about that. 'Why? Oh — don't you want to see me tonight? Have you changed your mind? I mean, I can go home now, of course . . . '

'Hey!' He laughed down at me. 'Of course I want to see you — I've been looking forward to it all day — it's just that something's come up tonight that I can't put off and I thought you might find it interesting.'

My beam spread from ear-to-ear. He still wanted to see me! So much for being cool and sophisticated!

'Okay — it — um — sounds intriguing.'

'You might find it a bit boring. I hope not, of course it depends what things you like doing, and I am really sorry about this not being a proper date. I promise that next time we'll go into the village and have a drink at the pub — or maybe you'd like to go to the cinema? I'd really like to see Midnight Cowboy, wouldn't you? Or we could go for a meal?'

Next time! He'd actually said there was going to be a next time! I wanted to turn cartwheels of sheer joy.

Oh, I'd love to do all those things — and especially with Lewis. I'd never done any of them before. It'd be like a real date. My first real date!

'Okay,' I said feeling far more confident, 'I'll hold you to that.'

Goodness, Paula would be so proud of me!

He fell into step beside me as we walked round the outskirts of Honey's massive boundary hedgerow, not seeming to mind too much that I hadn't held his hand. I wanted to! I wanted to hold his hand and cling on to it forever! But I couldn't — I couldn't hold his hand and shake like a leaf because then he'd know that he was my first boyfriend, and even worse, he'd know how I felt about him — and all the teenage magazines I'd read said the worst possible crime was letting a boy know you were keen.

'There's one thing I have to ask you before we plan any future dates though,' Lewis's eyes were suddenly serious. 'What about the boy you swore to love for ever and ever? Won't he object to you seeing me?'

Uh? I frowned. Which boy? I'd never sworn to love anyone for ever and ever and — oh! I remembered my RE text book and the declaration of devotion scribbled all over it. 'Nick Rayner is history,' I said, remembering being really impressed by a similar phrase that Paula had once used. 'He's just a boy from the village. I — er — don't see him any more. He's not my boyfriend.'

Well, at least that wasn't a lie . . .

'Good,' Lewis grinned, his eyes crinkling at the corners. 'You don't know how glad I am to hear it. So, have you been cloistered with those doom and gloom boys, Jeremiah and Isaiah, all day? Because if you have, you have my utmost admiration. I loathed studying.'

'What? Oh — er — yes . . . ' I didn't want anyone to know that I hadn't actually started my RE revision. Especially not Lewis. He might become all grown-up and suggest we deferred our date until after the exams were over. I quickly changed the subject. 'And I also got a Saturday job.'

'Really? Good for you. Where?'

So I told him about Sheldon Busby's, and he said he knew it and it was a great place, and we chatted about music and money and exams and life in general — and before I realised it my heart had stopped hammering and my palms had stopped sweating and I was really, really enjoying myself.

'What about you?' I asked as we

approached the back of Honeydew's mellow-bricked farmhouse, remembering the teenage mags advice that you should always appear interested in your boyfriend and ask him questions, too. Sadly it sounded like an interrogation. 'What have you been doing today?'

'Working on this project which is supposed to become my career. It's what I want you to see,' Lewis said, opening the gate in the tall hawthorn hedge, and standing back to let me through first. 'It's the reason I'm staying here. My parents have at last given up all hope of me doing what they want me to do, so they thought that if I stayed with Jess and Henry and actually tried to do something that I enjoyed and made a success of it, I may not be such a disappointment to them.'

I grinned to myself. Parents, it seemed, were parents the world over.

'Um — ' I stopped as we scrunched along Honeydew's wide gravelled paths. 'I know this sounds odd, but I'd really rather not meet your — um — godparents — at least, not tonight.'

'It doesn't sound odd at all,' Lewis said easily. 'Although I'm sure they'd love you — but I know what it's like being given the third degree. There'll be plenty of time to meet them later. To be honest, although they're sweethearts, they're a bit old-fashioned and they take their responsibilities as Godparents really seriously so think they have to keep an eye on me. Luckily I'm not living in the main house. They've given me one of the labourer's cottages in the yard.'

My heart started hammering again. He lived on his own. And he was taking me to his cottage. And I didn't know if I could trust him or not, but I was pretty sure I couldn't trust myself.

He laughed. 'My intentions are strictly honourable.'

I blushed. 'I'm sorry — I didn't mean . . . it's just — oh, I'm just being silly. Go on, tell me about this project — er — career.'

'I'll do better than that — I'll show you. It's in here.'

We'd passed the labourers' cottages and had reached one of the massive Dutch barns that were dotted around the Honeydew yard.

'After you,' Lewis gave a mock bow. 'Now you can see what it is I hope to do with my life . . . '

I stepped inside. It was cool and quite dark, and to start with all I could see were towering straw bales and stacked pallets of empty punnets. As my eyes became more used to the half-light I could make out some odd shapes at the far end, and then the lights flicked on and there seemed to be a crowd of people round a sort of stage, and then —

'Oh!!!' I looked up at him, my eyes shining. 'Oh, wow!'

7

I was speechless. It was like being Alice in Wonderland and discovering Santa's Grotto and Aladdin's Cave all rolled into one right here in Ashcote.

Lewis was beaming almost as broadly as I was. 'I thought, when you told me about your job in Sheldon Busbys, that we might just be on the same wavelength. Come and meet the others.'

I followed him across the barn towards the makeshift stage at the far end: a stage banked with towering stacks of black amplifiers and crisscrossed with a tangle of electrical wires and cables; a stage illuminated by coloured spotlights which glinted off microphone stands and sparkled on a huge gleaming silver drum kit and two very ornate electric guitars.

The four boys messing about with the musical instruments on the stage all turned and grinned at me and said hello.

'This is Clemmie,' Lewis said proudly. 'I'm sure you'll all be delighted to meet her at last seeing as I've talked about nothing or no-one else since yesterday.'

I sort of grinned back in a jaw-dropped way. They were gorgeous! All of them! None quite so gorgeous as Lewis, of course, but very, very nearly.

'Meet Solstice,' Lewis's voice was filled with laughter. 'Berkshire's answer to The Moody Blues, The Hollies and The Beach Boys — with a bit of originality thrown in — all rolled into one talented package. Close harmonies a speciality, but we're not averse to a few ballads or a bit of raunchy rock either. Jez there is our Svengali: he's our manager, accountant, roadie, electrician, sound and lighting expert, and he also drives the van. Vin's the drummer, Gus is our main vocalist, Berry's on lead guitar — and of course, there's the star of the show, me — vocals and the second greatest bass guitarist in the entire world after Bill Wyman.'

Giggling, I punched him playfully and he winked at me. My heart rocketed up into the stratosphere.

The other boys grinned a lot more and said hi and yeah, it's great to meet you at last and he's driven us mad by talking about you every spare minute and you're even more beautiful than he said you were — and I was in total heaven. Jenny and Dawn simply wouldn't believe it — and as for Paula — well!

'We've been offered our first ever professional gig in Cheltenham tomorrow night,' Lewis explained. 'Shortnotice, someone else dropped out — so we had to get together tonight for a final practice run — which is why we couldn't go to the pub.'

'This is much, much better than going to the pub,' I assured him, perching on a straw bale. 'Believe me.'

Lewis leaned down and kissed me very gently on the lips. I stared into his eyes and kissed him very gently and tentatively back. I was shaking. My mouth was dry. It was wonderful . . .

'You can be our critic,' he said softly, touching my face then straightening up and walking towards the stage. 'And you must be totally honest. If we're awful tell us, please, before we go public. This is a much sooner debut than we'd planned, but if you think we're okay then we'll go for it.'

I just nodded, hardly listening. I'd kissed him — and got it right!

I hugged my knees, watching in complete bliss as Lewis picked up his guitar, and along with the others, made sure all the electrical connections were okay and the microphones working.

When they started playing, as the first complex chords of the Moody Blues *Lovely to See You* billowed through the barn and soared roaring into the rafters, with Gus's strong voice sounding just like Justin Hayward and the others coming in in perfect close harmony, I was almost moved to tears. They not only looked wonderful, they sounded sensational. The music was loud, louder than any I'd ever heard, reverberating round the barn, and Lewis's insistent bass guitar throbbed into my very soul.

Beautiful song followed beautiful song. From tear-jerking ballads to hard rock, most of them were toe-tappingly familiar being Solstice's own interpretation of recent hits, but others were unknown to me, and I guessed they were the band's own compositions. They were word and note perfect, and extremely talented musicians.

'So . . . ' Lewis's voice echoed eerily through the microphone as the beat still thundered in echo in my ears, 'do you have any requests, Clemmie? A favourite song? Something you think will send them crazy in Cheltenham?'

'Well,' I knew I was blushing as they all looked down at me, 'my favourite song of all time is *Make It Easy On Yourself*, and I always wanted to buy the record but couldn't afford it at the time and now you can't get it — but I don't suppose . . . '

Solstice looked at one another and laughed. Lewis whistled. 'Spooky! That's one we've been rehearsing recently — we thought it would make a fab finale . . . so, just for you . . . '

Vin's drums dub-dub-dubbed into the familiar intro, while the guitars swept into the lush string melody, then, Lewis stepped up to the microphone . . .

Now, all these years on, I can still remember the tingle that shivered up and down my spine. Sitting on the hammock swing and closing my eyes it's as though a time machine has whisked me back through the years. I can still hear Lewis's deep, perfect voice as he sang those first heartbreaking words . . .

'Oh, breaking up is so very hard to do . . . '

I keep my eyes shut very tightly. I can hear my parents laughing across the garden at something they've found in the paper, but they sound as though

*they're miles away. Again, I'm trans-
ported back to that special time, that
special summer, simply by the words of
a song that is simply forever imprinted
in my head and in my heart. I remember that I cried then, and stupidly I'm
crying again now. The tears are sneaking from beneath my carefully mascared
lashes. I really must get a grip; can't let
Mum and Dad see. They'll wonder why
on earth I should be crying on this
happy day . . . I swallow and take a
deep breath. Amazing the power music
has on the emotions . . . Especially that
song. That song and the memories of
Lewis and that forbidden summer . . .*

As the last thrumming chords died
away, Lewis looked across at me from
the stage and pulled a face. 'So?'

'Brilliant,' I gulped back my tears.
'Absolutely totally, wonderfully, brilliant.'

The other boys laughed and looked
pleased and pretty exhausted all at the
same time. Lewis propped his guitar

against a speaker column and jumped off the makeshift stage.

'Do you think we're good enough to grace the Corn Exchange in Cheltenham tomorrow night, then?'

'More than good enough,' I laughed. 'They'll think they've got a Top 20 group on stage!'

'Which is, of course, what we're aiming to be,' Lewis sprawled beside me on the straw bale, and slid his arms round me. 'And if we make it, my parents may just forgive me for lousing up my academic career.'

The rest of the group joined us on the bales, passing round bottles of cider. I swigged at it along with the rest of them because I was hot and thirsty and because I wanted to. It was great — tasting of apples and honey and fizzed in my throat. It also made my head just slightly swimmy, and I giggled a lot and sang a very off-key version of *Good Morning Starshine* but no-one seemed to mind at all.

All the talk was of music, of bands, of

more music; the night air was sultry, warm and still, and through the open barn doors the sky was growing navy blue. It was summer in the Sixties and this was perfection. I had never been so happy in my entire life.

They had one more rehearsal of some of the trickier numbers, and what with the music and the effect of the cider and being hopelessly in love with Lewis and the whole darn heady atmosphere, I forgot to be shy and danced uninhibitedly on my straw bale, singing along.

'Clemmie's going to have to come with us,' Gus said as he pushed his mike back into the stand at the end of the session. 'Tomorrow night. To Cheltenham. We've never played so well — Clemmie'll have to be our mascot from now on. We can't go without her.'

Vin and Berry and Jez all whooped their agreement.

'Will all your girlfriends go, too?' I asked. It would be fun to make some new friends — meet girls who I hadn't known all my life. Girls who could talk about something other than A levels.

'No — we'd have to lay on a bus,' Jez laughed. 'These boys are serially unfaithful. Playing the field they like to call it. As for me — my girlfriend is at home in Bournemouth. I've been seeing her since we were at school. Now, Lewis here, he'd always said he was a field-player too. He was never going to fall into the lurve trap, although it seems as though you might have made him change his mind.'

'Too right,' Lewis jumped from the stage, hauled me to my feet and swung me round. 'From now on, Clemmie is definitely the only girl for me.'

Being swirled round by him added to the dizzying effect of the cider, and I felt as though I was flying and clung on to him, my arms tightly round his neck.

He pushed his face into my hair and his voice was muffled. 'And of course she's coming to Cheltenham with us tomorrow, or should, I say, with me. Just with me. Aren't you, Clemmie?'

Of course, I should have said no. I should have said it was out of the question. I should have said it was lovely to be asked but maybe next time . . . I should have said there were only five days before the first RE A level and I needed to revise. I should have said that going to Cheltenham on Friday night would make starting work at Sheldon Busbys at half-past eight on Saturday morning pretty difficult. I should have said there was no way on earth that my parents would allow me to go.

Those are the things I should have said.

8

I thought about all those things I should have said as I sat on Lewis's lap in the passenger seat of Solstice's transit van, bundling along the roads between Ashcote and Cheltenham the next night. I was really glad I hadn't said any of them. The radio was blaring from a single speaker perched on the dashboard: Steppenwolf's *Born To Be Wild*. It seemed so appropriate. This was bliss and I was young and alive — and there had to be more to life than Ashcote and home and school and exams and studying, always studying . . .

Mind you, I could have laughed at the appalling timing of it all. Shakespeare would have had a ball with the entire situation. It was all there: which wicked fate-fairy had deemed that I should meet the love of my life in the middle of the most important exams ever? Which benighted sprite had deemed that I should change in an instant from diligent swot to a teenager in love? Which accursed drowsy-potion had turned me overnight from a home-loving schoolgirl into a devious rock'n'roll groupie?

If only I'd met Lewis after the A levels then it would have been perfect — well, Mum and Dad would probably still have disapproved, but at least I'd have done my revision and taken my exams so he wouldn't have been classed as a distraction — but it must have been fate, and it had happened when it did, and now I couldn't and wouldn't change a thing.

Anyway, even if I had stayed at home I knew I wouldn't have been able to revise because the only thing I thought about was Lewis. He had taken over every one of my senses; he invaded my sleep; I spent all day smiling just because I could see his face in my mind, hear his voice, remember the things he'd said, the way he made me feel . . .

Mum and Dad had been pretty cross when I'd arrived home so late the night before. I'd felt terrible telling them that Jenny and I had been working hard on our revision notes, all the while trying not to giggle or grin too much or say something stupid because of the cider. And I hadn't been able to sleep; all I could hear was Solstice's wonderful music, and all I could think about was Lewis and the excitement he'd brought into my life. And yes, I'd felt guilty about lying to Mum and Dad, but it was only a tiny lie, wasn't it?

Once more using Jenny and the RE revision as an excuse, and foolishly promising to be home earlier, I'd hastily put on my make-up, worn my jeans and silver flip-flops again, this time with a filmy turquoise shirt, a jumble sale bargain, knotted at the waist, and met Lewis and the rest of the group at Honeydew at six o'clock. Having hidden my bike in the same place, I'd helped them load the equipment into the back of the dark blue van, feeling every inch the sort of rock chick I'd read about in Paula's Rave magazine.

I had no qualms at all about what I was doing. It was as if every romance I'd ever read, every adventure story I'd ever studied, had just leapt into wonderful, magical technicoloured life. I no longer had to live my Swinging Sixties vicariously through Paula and her tales — this was my moment — and it wasn't hurting anyone, was it?

'Sorry?' I looked up at Lewis as the transit van swung round a corner. 'What did you say?'

'I asked if your parents were okay with you coming out tonight?' Lewis tightened his arms around my waist. 'I mean, they probably think a jaunt like this will do you good before you start the rest of your exams, but maybe I should have met them, you know, explained that I'd take care of you and have you back in time for work in the morning.'

I bit my lip. I was getting quite good at deception. 'Oh, yes, they were fine about it — just fine.'

Jez looked across from the driving seat. 'If you hadn't have come with us tonight I'd've probably had to play bass. Lewis certainly wouldn't have gone without you.'

Gus, Berry and Vin, sitting shoulder-to-shoulder on the bench seat behind us laughed. The radio was now blaring out The Foundations: *In The Bad, Bad Old Days*. We sang along with the chorus.

'When did you all get together?' I asked in a quieter moment while Peter, Paul and Mary were singing poignantly about *Leaving On A Jet Plane*. 'Have you known each other for ages, or did you answer an advert in Melody Maker or something?'

'Nothing so romantic. We met at college,' Lewis said. 'We'd all joined one of the music clubs in the first year and formed Solstice initially just for fun, but none of us were particularly studious, and when we spent more time on the group than on lectures and tutorials, we decided to drop out and see if we had the talent to turn professional.'

'Your parents must have gone mad,' I shook my head, imagining what mine would have been like if I behaved in such a cavalier fashion with my academic future. 'I mean, we're so lucky, our generation, having opportunities to go to university and things that our parents never did. My dad drives a coach and my mum cleans at the local infant school and they're just so proud that I'm going to college.'

Lewis stroked my hair away from my face. 'Yeah, I can understand that. It wasn't quite like that for me — or for any of us really. Although my parents were furious that I wasn't going to follow in the family footsteps and become a doctor.'

My mouth went suddenly dry. Lewis's parents were *doctors*? Doctors, like all professional people, were regarded in Ashcote as being way above mere mortals. I'd never known anyone whose parents were doctors or lawyers or clergymen or anything like that. They were way out of my league, and my heart was sinking fast, but I wasn't going to show it.

'Um — that's nice — er — are they GPs? Er — locally?'

'Mum is, Dad's a neurosurgeon. Both in London. My brother and sister both studied medicine, too. I'm definitely the black sheep. We're all in the same boat though. Berry was reading law — his Dad's a QC, and Gus's father is in parliament, so he was reading politics and economics and — '

I swallowed a lump in my throat. I felt very stupid indeed. However much I pretended that it didn't matter, Lewis and the rest of Solstice were way, way above me socially. Different class, different worlds. It mattered very much indeed. I groaned. How could I have ever thought that Lewis with his looks and his talents and his social background, would feel anything for someone like me?

I had a sudden deep feeling of doom.

I think I already knew the answer to the next question, but I had to ask it. Had to know. 'Where were you at college? Which university?'

'Oxford,' Jez said, steering the transit into Cheltenham's main street. 'Dreaming spires, Commem Balls, punting on the Isis . . . Very swish, very privileged and very, very boring.'

I'd been right, of course. They were not only socially elite, they were the educational elite, too. And they were all wealthy enough for it not to matter at all that they'd thrown away the best educational opportunity the country could offer. I wanted to cry.

'There's the Corn Exchange,' Vin leaned over my shoulder and pointed. 'The organiser said if we went to the back entrance there'd be someone there to meet us.'

'Okay, Clemmie?' Lewis looked at me. 'You've suddenly gone very quiet.'

I nodded quickly. 'I'm fine. Really. Just a bit nervous, that's all.'

'Me too,' Lewis exhaled as Jez snaked

the van slowly up to a pair of battered green doors at the back of the Corn Exchange. 'I think I've got stage-fright . . .'

He needn't have worried. By the time Solstice had set up all their gear on stage, and Jez had fixed the speakers and the mikes and the swirling spotlights, and the compere, in his tuxedo, had whisked everyone up into a state of frenzy, it was like waiting for the start of a Rolling Stones concert.

Backstage, amongst the guitar cases and the clothes and towels and bottles and the heaps of musical paraphernalia, Lewis had kissed me and held me tight. As I was getting quite good at the mechanics of kissing, I'd kissed him back. Then I whispered my good lucks and tiptoed down the steps in the gloom to sit in the dance hall, out of sight at the side of the stage.

Beneath the multifaceted mirror-ball which rotated slowly in the ceiling, The Corn Exchange's packed audience was sprinkled with glittering diamonds in the darkness. Ten-deep, they'd crammed to the front of the stage, and the atmosphere was electric.

'Ladies and gentlemen!' the compere screamed. 'The biggest musical phenomena in the Southern Hemisphere! I know you can't wait any longer — so you won't have to! For the first time in Cheltenham — let's hear it for — Solstice!'

The curtains swished back as Vin gave a thunderous drum roll and the lights criss-crossed backwards and forwards across the stage. Lewis, Berry and Gus, so tall and slim and gorgeous in their tight jeans and tie-dye T-shirts, stepped up to their microphones and roared into the Hollies' *Stay*.

The girls, all dressed in hippie layers with flowers in their hair, or little Clodagh Rogers mini dresses, screamed like banshees at the sight of so much sexy male beauty.

I didn't blame them. I sat in the darkness, totally mesmerised.

Solstice were sensational. I stared at

Lewis, playing his guitar and singing up on the stage, not quite believing that he was mine. Well, for tonight anyway. My hopes of forever had been dashed the moment I'd happily blurted out about my working class background and ruined everything. But right now, that didn't matter. If I never saw Lewis again after tonight, being here, being part of this, was worth every bit of heartbreak it would cause in the future. This moment, I knew, was something I'd remember for the rest of my life.

They swept triumphantly from one superb song into the next, and the Corn Exchange rocked. I felt superbly smug, sitting there in the shadows, watching as the girls screamed and yelled and danced and preened in front of the stage. They could look all they wanted — but I'd be the one going home in the van.

'Now we're going to slow things down a bit for the end of the set to let you lovebirds have a smoochy dance or two,' Gus's voice echoed from the microphone, 'and I'm going to hand over lead vocal to Lewis here on bass guitar. The song is *Make It Easy On Yourself* by The Walker Brothers, one of our favourites . . . ' he paused, laughing, as everyone roared their approval. 'And obviously one of yours, too — which is just as well. And this one — ' he glanced across to where I was sitting, 'I've been told, is just for Clemmie.'

The lights dimmed, the arousing intro started and Lewis stepped up to the microphone, strumming the bass line. His voice was deep, pure and spine-tingling. His eyes never left mine. It was as if no-one else was in the room. The words, heartbreakingly romantic, were simply from him to me. I sat and shivered, holding my hand over my mouth so as not to let any sound escape, and felt my eyes fill with tears.

So this was love? Always and forever.

When it was over I simply smiled at him, shaking, applauding with everyone else, then Solstice moved on to their slow, smoochy numbers and I sat, transfixed. My world had been tumbled upside down. Everything had changed. All the things that I'd taken for granted had been turned on their head. Nothing would ever be the same again.

All too soon it was over. The Corn Exchange audience roared for more, and Solstice gave them a quick encore, then it was a frantic dash to clear everything away and load the van. There was no time to speak to Lewis, only a moment to give him a hug and the briefest of kisses and ask unspoken questions with my eyes. I was furiously jealous of the dozens of giggling girls who hung around as we were clearing up, all flirting and asking silly questions, and writing their addresses and some phone numbers on bits of paper.

Eventually, after umpteen trips backwards and forwards, our arms loaded with gear, the van was packed, and my head still reverberated with the echoes of the songs. Berry and Gus and Vin had to be prised away from three of the local girls who had along with several others, rather childishly I thought, scrawled their names and messages of undying love all over the transit in lipstick.

'Fantastic,' Jez said in delight, waving a fistful of pound notes as we all scrambled into the van and slammed the doors. 'They even paid us a bonus — and they want us back and I've got half a dozen other contacts who want bookings in the next month — and I think, just think, we might be on our way.'

He roared the transit into life, turned up the radio and we zoomed away from Cheltenham.

'Told you Clemmie would bring us good luck, didn't I?' Gus's voice was hoarse. 'We won't be able to go anywhere without her now.'

'Lewis won't anyway,' Berry laughed. 'They're joined at the hip. Which leaves all those girls free for us! Did you see the redhead in the white dress? Wow!'

'She fancied me, not you!' Vin

croaked. 'And I've got her phone number!'

'No way!' Gus interrupted. 'They all fancied me because I'm the singer!'

They were all as high as kites. Buzzing with adrenaline and success. I was much the same. I'd never known life could be so wonderful, so different, so exciting. Even if it wasn't going to last.

'So . . . ' Lewis tightened his arms around me. 'Did you enjoy it?'

'It was amazing. The most amazing night of my life . . . Thank you . . . Oh, and — and for *Make It Easy On Yourself*. It was . . . It was . . . '

'It'll be our song from now on,' Lewis kissed my throat in the darkness as the van rocked, speeding away from the town and into the countryside. 'Not that we're ever going to break up, are we?'

'Never, ever,' I pressed my cheek against his chest in the darkness. The radio was playing Jimi Hendrix's *Purple Haze*. 'I think I must be the luckiest and happiest person in the entire world tonight.'

'Joint luckiest and happiest,' Lewis turned my face to his and kissed me. 'We're going to be just great together.'

I gave a huge sigh of relief. He still wanted to see me. Even though we were oceans apart in just about every way possible. Whatever he said, it wouldn't last, of course. It couldn't possibly work out. But tonight I wasn't going to think of the maybes. Tonight I was just going to enjoy every minute. And I'd enjoy every minute until the minutes ended and then my heart would break.

'I don't think I'll ever sleep tonight,' I murmured. 'Right now, I feel as though I'll never sleep again.'

Lewis laughed softly. 'Great, isn't it? A million times better than swotting to be a doctor anyway — and I hate to say this, but you're going to be mighty tired for your first day at work.'

I shook my head happily, feeling his hair silky on my skin. 'Oh, I'll just have to try to calm down. I'll make a milky drink when I get home and read something boring like my RE notes — they're better than any sleeping pills. Don't worry, I'll be okay after a night's sleep.'

'There's not much of the night left, Clemmie. We're nowhere near Ashcote yet, and it's already half-past two.'

9

'Drop me here, please,' I said, my heart in my boots as Jez eventually steered the transit through the dark shadows of Ashcote's main road. 'This'll be fine.'

It was nearly half past three in the morning. I couldn't go all the way back to Honeydew to collect my bike then cycle home. It'd have to wait.

'Are you sure?' Lewis wouldn't let me go. 'It's dark. This can't be where you live and — look, I know you said your parents were okay about you coming with us, but none of us thought we'd be this late. Will they be waiting up for you? I think I ought to come with you and explain.'

'No, no.' I shook my head quickly. 'No, they won't be waiting up for me. It'll be fine.'

Oh, what a tangled web I'd woven!

'Well, at least let us drop you at your

door.' Lewis looked concerned. 'We can't just leave you here in the pitch dark. There aren't any street lights or anything.'

'I'll be home in a couple of ticks from here,' I fumbled with the door catch. 'The village is as safe as houses — ah!' I opened the door, kissed Lewis briefly, said goodnight to the others and jumped out on to the road.

'But, when will I see you again?' Lewis leaned from the van. 'I don't know where you live, you're not on the phone — Clemmie, please . . . '

'I'll get in touch tomorrow — um — later today. At Honeydew. And thank you so much for tonight. For everything. I'll never, ever forget it. Goodnight.'

And not looking back, I ran through Ashcote's darkness. In half an hour the dawn would start to streak the sky with light. I just prayed and prayed that Mum and Dad would be in bed.

They weren't. All the lights were on. I pushed the back door open, feeling like a criminal. All the wonderful, heady excitement of the evening had evaporated. They were sitting at the kitchen table, still fully dressed, Mum was crying, Dad just looked exhausted.

I felt bitterly ashamed. 'I'm so sorry I'm late . . . '

They jumped up, shouting at the same time, upset and angry. I said nothing.

Their words tumbled over themselves: they'd been to Jenny's, they knew I hadn't been there on either night; Dawn hadn't seen me; not even Paula had any idea where I'd gone. Then there were loud accusations of telling lies, of worrying them to death; they'd scoured the village when I hadn't come home by midnight and they'd discovered my bike was gone. Then came the tears and the we've done everything for you, trusted you, given up so much . . .

It was awful. Truly awful. I knew I deserved every bit of it.

'Look — I'm so sorry — I got

delayed. I know you're upset — I knew you'd be worried but I couldn't let you know I was going to be late. But I'm okay. Really.'

Dad was more angry than I'd ever seen him in my life. 'And how were we supposed to know that? We thought you were dead! We imagined all sorts of things! Where the hell have you been?'

Mum just burst into noisy tears again. I wanted to cuddle her but thought she'd push me away and I couldn't bear it. I hated them being so angry with me. They'd never ever been really cross with me before, at least not at the same time — I'd spent 17 years with the best and kindest parents in the world — and simply by doing something a little bit foolish that had made me happy I'd reduced them to this state of distraught fury.

But I knew I couldn't tell them where I'd been. If I told them then they'd forbid me from ever seeing Lewis again. I just shook my head, blinking away my own tears. 'I went out . . . with some friends . . . I needed to have a break from studying. I'm really, really sorry.'

'Sorry isn't good enough! What friends? Why weren't you revising? Where have you been until this time of night? Dear God — ' Mum dabbed at her eyes. 'You haven't been with Nick Rayner, have you?'

Again, I said nothing. I really wanted to laugh and say that Nick Rayner was the last bloke on earth I'd stay out half the night for, and that I'd spent the last two evenings in the company of the only boy I'd ever love, who just happened to be an ex-Oxford under-grad and whose father was a neurosurgeon — but I knew that they'd think I was mocking them.

'She has!' Dad jumped to the same conclusion, clearly taking my silence as an admission of guilt. 'Oh, Clemmie! How could you do this to us? After everything we've taught you? Warned you about? What on earth possessed you . . . ?'

I sniffed back my tears. This was

terrible. 'All I can say is sorry. I would have let you know where I was, but without a phone and — '

'But two nights on the trot!' Dad roared. 'You've lied to us, Clemmie! Deliberate lies! Why on earth would you do that? We trusted you — and — this must never happen again. Understand?'

I nodded. I felt bone tired. I just wanted to curl up in bed and pull the eiderdown over my head and make all this go away.

'You've let us down,' Mum had stopped crying which was a blessing. 'That's what you've done. We had such great hopes for you — you were going to be different, going away to university, having a chance . . . now you're no better than Paula!'

'Oh, Mum, please don't say things like that! Yes, I've worried you and upset you tonight — but I'm still going to university. I'm still the same person — and yes, okay, I know I was thoughtless and stupid — but I haven't murdered anyone, or done anything wrong. I was just enjoying myself and being a bit selfish and silly. I'm safe and I'm home and it won't happen again, I promise. Now, please, please can we just go to bed? You must be exhausted and I've got to start at Sheldon Busbys in about three hours time.'

For a moment they looked as though Sheldon Busbys was the last place I'd be going, but perhaps they thought that I'd be out of Nick Rayner's clutches behind a shop counter. I didn't even hang around to say goodnight properly, but with a further flurry of mumbled apologies, flew out of the kitchen.

'One more thing, Clemmie!' Dad's voice bellowed along the hall. 'You're not to see that Rayner yob again, understood?'

I paused at the bottom of the stairs. If I hadn't felt so deflated and awful I'd have probably smiled. Still, at least this time I wouldn't have to lie to anyone. 'Yes, Dad. I promise I'll never, ever go out with Nick Rayner again.'

10

Starting a new job while half-asleep and mind-blowingly in love was not to be recommended. Fortunately it was Paula's Saturday off so I didn't have her asking probing questions all day. Sheldon Busbys was enough of an ordeal as it was. I'd pulled on my jeans and the black and silver shirt and let my hair hang loose as there was no time before catching the bus to do anything with it. My eyes were gritty, my head ached and all I wanted to do was curl up in a dark corner and go to sleep.

Mr Smithson was very kind, as were Julie and Viv, the other two Saturday assistants who made up the staff with four full-timers. They showed me how to work the till, how to place the records on the turntables for the listening booths, and how to find the index numbers of the LPs when customers brought the empty sleeves to the counter and slip the right record inside.

I tried to remember everything. 'What if it's a record we haven't got?'

'If you get asked for something you can't find,' Mr Smithson said, 'you look it up in these reference folders. A lot of records are old and no longer easily available, or perhaps foreign imports not generally released over here, but we can order them. Never turn a customer away. Always make a sale. You'll soon get the hang of it. Go on try it out . . . '

Of course I tried it out on *Make It Easy On Yourself*. I'd already decided that it would be the very first thing I'd buy with my wages. And I'd play it over and over and over again.

'Oh! It's not listed — not as a single any more — only on an LP — and — ' The disappointment swamped me. 'It costs — oh, and look how much it costs to order it!'

Mr Smithson laughed. 'When people want a record for their collection the cost is usually immaterial. Anyway, you seem to have picked that up quickly. Clever girl — I do hope you'll enjoy working here.'

I did. It was frantically busy, and hard work, and the morning flew by. I was tired, and missing Lewis, and guilty about upsetting my parents, and worried about the RE exam — but it was great to be meeting people, listening to music all day long, and knowing that I'd be paid at half past five. But more than any of that I was reliving, over and over, the previous night in my head. Every detail, every word, every touch, every kiss. It was bliss.

By lunch time I'd lost track of the number of people who had come in to listen to and then buy *Something In The Air* by Thunderclap Newman. It was number one that week and I felt that the words would be branded on my brain until I died.

'Can we listen to *Something in the Air* by — '

'Thunderclap Newman,' I finished

for what seemed like the millionth time, without looking up. 'Yes, hold on . . . um — booth number 4 will be free in a moment — oh!'

Jenny and Dawn were grinning at me from the other side of the counter.

'We don't really want to buy it,' Jenny said. 'We've only come in to find out about you and Nick Rayner.'

'Your Mum was livid last night,' Dawn's eyes were wide with delight. 'It was great.'

'You look really, really rough,' Jenny said with relish. 'Which is all you deserve seeing as you dropped me right in it. Why didn't you say you'd told them you were with me?'

'I'm so sorry — I know I should have warned you, but there wasn't time — and how was I know I'd be late and they'd check up on me?'

'What was it like, though?' Dawn clearly wasn't bothered about the moral ethics involved. 'What was he like? Where did you go? What did you do? Are you seeing him again?'

I tried, and failed, to stop myself from smiling. They completely misinterpreted the smile.

'Oh!' Jenny practically stamped her foot. 'Oh, it's not fair!!!'

'I can't believe you've been out with him!' Dawn groaned. 'You are soooo lucky!'

From the corner of my eye I could see Mr Smithson watching me, so I plonked Thunderclap Newman on the turntable and ushered Jenny and Dawn towards booth 4. 'Go on, I can't talk now — I'll lose my job. Maybe I'll see you later.'

They both shook their heads.

'Can't. We're doing revision all weekend. I suppose you've finished yours?'

'Not really.' That was an understatement! 'I'm going to get stuck into it tonight and do nothing else for the next couple of days. Still, once Tuesday is over we'll have more time to catch up.'

'Yeah, then we'll want all the sordid details. You are such a sly maggot,

Clemmie Long! I'd much rather have been with Nick than reading about the industrial revolution.' Dawn, whose history exam was on Tuesday morning too, looked pea-green with envy.

Jenny nodded. 'At least we'll have a bit of breathing space after Tuesday — until the second RE paper the next week — and yukky History of Art.'

'Clemmie! There are a lot of people still waiting to be served!' Mr Smithson's voice bellowed across the top of Marmalade's *Baby Make It Soon*. 'And you've still got an hour until your break! Come along! Chop-chop!'

By quarter past five I thought I'd fall asleep on my aching feet. I had never been so tired in my life. I had an evening of revision to face but all I wanted to do was sleep, after I'd seen Lewis, of course.

'Clemmie — there's a gentleman asking about an out of press record,' Mr Smithson called along the counter just as we were closing. 'Can you look it up for him, please?'

Wearily, easing my feet behind the counter, I reached for the folders. 'Yes, certainly. What's the title?'

'*Make It Easy On Yourself*, of course.'

I looked up straight into Lewis's blue eyes. Well, almost. Most of his face was hidden behind a huge bunch of turquoise carnations.

'Oh . . . ' I was almost overcome by the rush of love I felt for him.

He laughed gently, handing me the flowers. 'Yes, I feel a bit like that, too. These are for you — I thought they'd match your eyes. There's a shop in the market that dyes them every colour under the sun.'

'Thank you,' I bit my lip and blinked back the tears. Crying would be very childish. 'They're gorgeous — and no-one has ever bought me flowers before, not even ordinary ones, and these aren't and — and oh, thank you . . . '

'You can get away now, Clemmie,' Mr Smithson was beaming. 'You've done really well today. Here's your money, my dear and thank you. I hope you and your young man have a lovely evening.'

I think I floated out of the shop. Outside, it was noisy and stiflingly hot; the heat from the late afternoon sun beating down to meet the fumes of the busy street rushing up. Just like *Summer In the City*.

'I hope you don't mind roughing it in the transit,' Lewis took my flower-free hand and pulled me towards him and kissed me. 'I would have collected you in my car but Berry's borrowed it as his brakes have gone — again — so I've pinched the van from Jez. I knew you'd be tired and I thought you should be chauffeured home in style.'

And I was. And I much preferred travelling in Solstice's van than in Lewis's car, I decided. I'd guessed on the day we met that he had a car. They must all have cars. They were so rich and privileged that having cars was an accepted part of their lifestyle. I didn't tell him that very few people in our street owned a car. That Dad, with a horror of buying things on hire-purchase, had worked overtime to save for a car for years, but that the car fund had become my university fund two years ago. The social gulf between us was wide enough. It didn't need added illustration.

All tiredness forgotten, I sat in the front seat of the transit, my feet up on the dashboard, the flowers in my lap and my hand under Lewis's on the steering wheel.

He asked me if my parents had been angry at my late return, and I lied again, so easily, and said no. He asked me if I was okay about my RE exam and if my revision was on schedule. I lied and said yes. He told me that Jez had spent all day phoning the people who had shown interest in Solstice the night before, as well as contacting other venues across the country, and that firm bookings were coming in thick and fast.

I was so pleased for him. For them. For me, too.

'Home or Honeydew?' Lewis asked

as we reached Ashcote.

'Honeydew, please. My bike's still under the hedge.'

'Do you have to go straight home?'

Yes, of course I did. My RE revision simply couldn't wait any longer. I shook my head. 'Not straight away.'

Honeydew basked under the almost-midsummer sun. The fields were still filled with fruit pickers, and as we drove through the main gates I ducked down, pretending to collect my flowers together, just in case Mr Leach spotted me.

We stopped in the high-walled courtyard outside the labourers' cottages. Lewis caught me as I jumped out of the van. 'I bet you could do with a long, cold drink.'

'I'd love one,' I clutched my flowers as he took my hand and led me into his cottage. 'It seems years since lunch time — oh, wow! This is fabulous!'

The cottage was low-ceilinged and very tiny; it was almost impossible to believe that fifty years earlier whole families of six or seven people had lived happily in these three small rooms. It was simply but expensively furnished, with white curtains, dark red leather sofa and chairs, a television and an extensive hi-fi system. There were ornately patterned rugs on the quarry tiled floors, and Lewis's beloved Rickenbacker guitar was propped against one of the walls, the case open beside the television set, sheet music strewn across the coffee table.

'I've been working on some fiddly bits. We write some of our own songs. Well I do most of the music — Gus and Berry write the lyrics — just clear a space to sit down.' Lewis disappeared into the kitchen. 'Iced coffee okay?'

I said yes. I'd never had iced coffee in my life but guessed it was something upper class people had on hot days.

We had our iced coffee in little glass cups. It tasted like nectar. The doors and windows of the cottage were open, and across the courtyard the golden fields and orchards of Honeydew stretched away as far as the eye could see, melting into a blue haze in the skyline.

'I've got something else for you,' Lewis walked across to the stereo. 'I bought this in America when it first came out and found it this morning — '

He'd been to *America*? I was speechless with admiration. He'd probably flown on one of the brand new jumbo jets — or maybe even on that space-age Concorde. Of course he'd probably been everywhere, done everything, while I . . . The opening bars of *Make It Easy On Yourself* suddenly flooded richly into the cottage and it didn't matter how wide the cultural gulf was. Not any more.

Smiling, Lewis curled against me on the sofa, pulled me into his arms and kissed me.

Two hours later, I cycled home in a complete dream. The turquoise carnations were in my basket, *Make It Easy On Yourself* was in my bag, in my head, and forever in my heart, and the fact that I had only two days before the RE exam didn't seem to matter at all. Nothing mattered. Just Lewis and being in love.

By Tuesday morning nothing had changed. I couldn't eat, had slept only fitfully, dreamed of Lewis constantly and hadn't been able to concentrate for more than thirty seconds on Isaiah and Jeremiah. Mum and Dad seemed delighted that I'd come home relatively early after Sheldon Busbys, had believed me that Mr Smithson had bought me the flowers as a welcome-to-the-staff present, and put my trance-like state down to pre-exam nerves. They even accepted the fact that I spent every moment in my bedroom playing *Make It Easy On Yourself* over and over again as a sign that I was diligently swotting.

'Okay?' Dawn asked as we walked towards the school in the early morning sun. 'How do you think you'll do?'

I shook my head. There was no way on earth I'd tell anyone that I had done nowhere near enough revision. 'It'll depend on the questions. I'm hoping I'll pick up marks on the second paper if this one is awful. Oh, it'll be okay . . . '

'Course it will,' Jenny gave a little skip. 'You're naturally clever. Everyone says you'll sail through them even if you never opened a book. And after all, you've got love to see you through, haven't you?'

'*What?*'

Dawn stuck her tongue out at me. 'Bet you wish that you were doing Nick Rayner for A levels, don't you? I know I do — oh, what does she want?'

Paula Conway, in the skimpiest white skirt and a little pink top, was sitting on the wall again.

'Hiya, kiddies! Back to school?' She looked at my rucked up uniform dress and my stupid straw boater and laughed. 'And you are a right dark horse, Clem. Mr Smithson thinks you're the bee's knees — *and* I hear you're going out with Nick! Still waters or what?'

I felt very little-girlie beside her painted sophistication, but I smiled. 'Yes, well, some of us have it, some of us don't. Anyway, why aren't you at work?'

'Going in at lunch time. I told Mr Smithson I had a dental appointment. Whereas actually my appointment is much more interesting than that.'

I laughed. 'Oh, Mr Wonderful, is it? Managed to shake off his wife and kids for the morning, has he? Sorry, can't stop — have a nice time.'

I held my hat on as I ran to catch up with Jenny and Dawn and the rest of the nervously giggling girls who were streaming round a couple of parked cars towards the school gates. Paula was welcome to her clandestine affair with her mystery man. I had the real thing . . .

Dawn stopped walking and grabbed my arm. 'Holy Moses! Look at him!'

'Blimey!' Jenny choked. 'Pinch me and tell me I'm dreaming — he is *gorgeous* . . .'

Lewis was leaning against the school gates.

I wanted to laugh out loud. Snatching my hat from my head, I ran towards him. He caught me and swung me round.

'Oh, Clemmie — I've missed you so much. It's been driving me crazy, not seeing you. And you look really cute . . . I had to see you — just to say good luck and to give you this.'

He handed me a small square box. Aware that most of the Sixth Form were watching with open-mouthed envy, I reached up and kissed him. So much for being discreet!

'You'll never know how much I've missed you.' Shakily, I opened the box. Two slender silver bangles nestled in tissue paper. 'Oh, Lewis, they're lovely. Thank you so much.'

'One for luck and one for love,' Lewis slid them on my wrist. 'Mind you, if your school is anything like mine was they'll confiscate them — but hey, it's worth the risk. Anyway, all the luck in the world with the exam and I'll see you later.'

'It'll have to be after the exams are over.'

He kissed me again. 'I can't wait that long!'

'I'm not sure I can, either . . . oh, I'll have to go and I don't want to . . . '

We shared one last lingering kiss. In a total daze I pulled reluctantly away from him, took one last look, then ran through the school gates. Dawn and Jenny and everyone else bombarded me with questions. I didn't answer, didn't listen to them. I knew then that I'd smile for ever and ever. I was simply walking on air.

Stroking the bangles, I turned round again, just for one last look at him before the RE exam took over the next three hours of my life, and nearly passed out.

Outside the school gates Lewis was opening the driver's door of a gleaming black Ford Capri, and Paula was scrambling into the passenger seat.

11

I felt numb. Completely dead. I ignored everyone's excited questions about Lewis as we queued to file into the assembly hall. It was as though I wasn't there. Everything was happening at the end of a long, black tunnel. My legs wobbled alarmingly and my chest hurt so much I could scarcely breathe.

And of course, once we were in the exam room and I turned the paper over, I couldn't answer a single question. Even if the print hadn't been blurred by my tears I wouldn't have been able to write a sensible word. So much for me being able to pass exams without revising. Even without the shock of discovering that Lewis was Paula's Mr Wonderful, I knew I simply hadn't done enough work.

I really didn't care. The pain inside was indescribable. It all made awful sense now: Paula and her mystery man who came into Sheldon Busby's and did other things in the evenings and who drove a Ford Capri. Paula's lover who was so beautiful, so educated, so rich . . . I felt sick. Lewis probably had a whole stack of suitable records and bangles and a standing order for dyed-carnations. He probably laughed himself silly by making fools of the local girls. I was just the current link in a never-ending chain of working class dalliances.

For three hours these thoughts and others far more awful hammered through my brain. For three hours I stared at the questions and stabbed at my paper with the nib of my fountain pen. For three hours I wrote rubbish and thought about Lewis and Paula together and wanted to die.

'Five minutes to go, girls,' the invigilator warned. Then, 'that's it. Time's up. Stop writing. Make sure your name is on all the sheets.' She stalked down from the stage and marched up and down the rows. 'Clementine Long! You know very well that jewellery is forbidden in school! Take those bracelets off and I don't want to see them again!'

'Yes miss,' I nodded. I didn't ever want to see them again, either.

I knew I'd throw them away when I got home, along with the carnations and the record and one of Lewis's old plectrums I'd picked up in the cottage — Paula probably had a matching set, too. Half the girls in Ashcote were probably the proud possessors of Lewis's gifts.

Not waiting for Jenny and Dawn and their never-ending questions, I belted out of the exam room and ran home. Muttering to Mum that the exam had been awful, I flew upstairs, hurled myself on to my bed and cried as though my heart would break. Which of course, it already had.

I'm not sure how I survived the next few days. They all merged into a sort of blur of pain. Mum and Dad put it down to my studying too much and blamed themselves for having such high expectations. They even thought they may have been a bit too harsh about my escapade with Nick. I simply looked at them through my swollen eyes and couldn't tell them the truth. The truth and I seemed to have parted company ages ago.

I didn't want to see anyone. I didn't even go to work at Sheldon Busbys on Saturday. How could I? Paula would be there. I asked Mum to ring from the phone box at the Ashcote Stores and apologise to Mr Smithson. She told him I had a sick headache and he was apparently so upset that it made me cry even more.

I didn't go downstairs when Dawn and Jenny called round. I did nothing but watch the sun burn its way across the sky and the darkness eventually fall and stared unseeing at my text books. *Make It Easy On Yourself* languished silent on my Dansette turntable, the turquoise carnations died in their vase, and the silver bangles were with the plectrum beneath my pillow. I would throw them all away one day — but not yet.

On two occasions Paula came round to see me but my shriek of fury made Mum explain to her that I wasn't feeling too good and she went away again.

Somehow, because I had to, I went in for the last two exams. I needn't have bothered. The second RE paper was as abysmal as the first, and as for History of Art . . .

Dawn and Jenny, now completely mystified about my prolonged headache, my woebegone state, Nick Rayner, and the identity of the boy at the gates, asked various probing questions. I snapped my answers, none of them true of course, and returned to skulking in my bedroom.

'Will you feel up to going into the record shop tomorrow?' Mum asked, sitting on my bed, trying to tempt me with a cucumber sandwich. 'Or do you want me ring them again?'

I shook my head. It didn't matter. Nothing mattered. I'd have to face Paula eventually and Lewis Coleman-Beck wouldn't be so brazen or so cruel to come into the shop while we were both there, would he?

'No, I'll go in tomorrow. Mum — I'm really, really sorry about everything.'

She cuddled me, not understanding why I was apologising. 'Maybe some fresh air would do you good, love. Why don't you do a bit more fruit picking up at Honeydew?'

'No! Oh, Mum . . . '

'It's all right, Clemmie, love. It's all right. We've put far too much pressure on you. You'll be fine now those awful old exams are out of the way. Look, I'll talk to your Dad and if you really want to go out with Nick then maybe we can sort something out and — '

'I don't!' I shook my head. 'I don't want to go out with stupid Nick Rayner or any other boy ever! I'll never, ever go out with anyone again!'

Mum, looking even more worried patted my shoulder. 'I blame myself for this — but I only wanted what was best for you. For you to have a better chance in life than I had. You've worked so hard — and when you're at university you'll have years of studying. You should get out and enjoy yourself while you can.'

I threw myself into her arms and sobbed. I wanted to tell her it wasn't her fault at all; I wanted to tell her everything but I couldn't. She didn't understand and just kept saying it would be all right. But I knew it wouldn't. Nothing would ever be all right again.

The next morning I caught the early bus into Reading. There was no way on earth that I wanted to make the journey with Paula, although there was some demon nagging at me telling me she'd probably be getting a lift in the Ford Capri anyway.

Mr Smithson was delighted to see me, asked kindly about my headache and the exams, and then left me alone. Which was just as well. I had to cope with this on my own. Other people, I told myself, had survived broken hearts and so would I.

Paula arrived at just after nine. I couldn't look at her. I hated her. She'd probably come straight from Lewis's cottage. I heard her giving Mr Smithson some excuse and then them both laughing. I hoped they weren't laughing at me.

Every record I played was about lost love. Every customer that morning seemed to want to listen to *I'll Never Fall In Love Again* by Bobbie Gentry. The words went round and round in my head and I hated them. They were all so painfully true.

'Feeling better?' Paula asked as we both reached for the same LP. 'I came round a couple of times to see how your exams had gone, but your Mum said — '

'I'm fine thank you.' I gritted my teeth. 'Absolutely fine. And you can tell that to Mr Wonderful — or shall we give him his real name now?'

Paula shrugged. 'Why would he be interested? And you can call him what you like — he's in the past. We finished last week. And no, before you say anything, he's not married, but he is a two-timing rat. Still — it's his loss.' She fluttered her batwing eyelashes across the counter. 'Yes, sir — we've got all the Bee Gees records. Over here . . . '

I took the money from my customer and fumed. So Lewis had dumped Paula had he? How long would I have lasted if I hadn't found out? And was he three or even four timing us both? I groaned in misery. So much for the for ever and ever love I'd dreamed about.

'One thing,' Paula hissed as she pushed past to get to the till. 'I went out with Nick Rayner — yeah, okay I know what I said about him, but at least me and Nick are on the same wavelength — last night and he swears he's never been out with you in his life.'

'He hasn't. I lied. I've lied about a lot of things.'

'*You?*' Paula look shocked. 'Miss Goody Two Shoes? You tell *lies?*'

'Hundreds,' I nodded. 'Cut out the acting, Paula. You know I've been lying about everything. You must do. After all — you've been seeing Lewis, too.'

'Lewis?' She frowned at me. 'Lewis who? Oh, *Lewis!* Oooooh — if only! He is simply fab! And what do you mean 'too'? Good God — you mean *you* — *you're* Lewis's girlfriend?'

It was all getting a bit Alice Through the Looking Glass.

Paula grabbed my arm and dragged me out from behind the counter. 'There's a problem with the speakers in booth 2,' she shouted to Mr Smithson, as she pulled me through the shop. 'We're just going to sort it out.'

'Okay,' she shut the door. 'Now let's get a few things straight here . . . '

It took several false starts. We both talked at the same time. But slowly, slowly, the tangles became unravelled.

I shook my head in total disbelief. 'So, you hadn't met Lewis at all until that morning outside the school?'

'No — Berry was always very careful to keep me well away from his friends and his whole life. I didn't even know he was in a group until Lewis told me. I just saw the car, the Capri which Berry said was his, outside the school and thought it was Berry because we were supposed to be meeting. Then when it wasn't, I asked your Lewis if he knew where Berry was as he hadn't turned up — and he took me to Berry's flat in Lower Ashcote.' Paula shook her head. 'I felt so stupid — I didn't even know where Berry lived. He'd never told me. And when we got there Berry was with another girl — I think Lewis was as shocked as me — and I told him I didn't share my men, and he just laughed, and Lewis drove me back home . . . And that's it.' Paula chewed her lip and sighed a bit. 'Berry's just a lowlife womaniser, but so gorgeous with it, and I fell for all his charms and lies.'

Berry often borrowed Lewis's Capri when his own car was off the road. I knew that. Lewis had told me.

I wanted to kiss Paula. I wanted to kiss the entire universe.

Paula smiled at me. 'Anyway, all Lewis did on both journeys was talk about you — except I didn't know it was you. He didn't name names. I was soooo jealous — he is simply sensational. He did say you were at the Grammar School and he wouldn't be seeing you until after the exams were over — but even then I didn't twig. I thought it was probably Pammie Mason, you know, the Sixth Form's answer to Lulu.'

I tried to stop myself beaming from ear to ear and failed.

Paula looked at me in admiration. 'So you've been seeing Lewis all this time and no-one knew? Not even your parents? Wow, Clemmie, you're amazing.'

I told her all of it then. The lies I'd told to absolutely everyone. And why.

'You're mad,' she pulled a face. 'Lewis is gaga about you. He wouldn't care what your Dad does for a job or where you lived or anything. Believe me, I know when a bloke's in love — and he is — and as for the rest of it — I can't believe you thought your Mum and Dad wouldn't approve.'

'They wouldn't have though. They would have even disapproved of Prince Charles asking me out during the exams.' I groaned. 'Oh God, Paula — I've really messed up my exams, and now they'll blame Lewis and they'll never like him, so I still can't tell them about him and — oh, I've been such a fool.'

'We're all fools when it comes to love,' Paula said, sounding about a hundred and ninety three. 'But yeah, probably best not to introduce Lewis to your parents yet then, just in case. And I'll warn Dawn and Jenny to keep their mouths shut about him, too. Mind, you'll probably sail through the exams anyway, but even if you don't, you can take them again, can't you? You can just start university a term late or something — don't worry Clem — you'll be fine.'

I nodded. I would be. The world was suddenly a wonderful, wonderful place.

I skipped back into the shop, and sang along with *I'll Never Fall In Love Again*. Huh, I thought, what did Bobbie Gentry know anyway? She'd obviously not met the right boy for her yet. Whereas I . . .

When I got home after Sheldon Busbys, Mum and Dad were just so delighted that I was feeling better and back to normal, that they thought going for a bike ride sounded just the ticket. The bike ride, in the low, hot evening sun, took me — of course — to Honeydew.

Lewis, wearing faded Levis and a white T-shirt, was sitting on the cobbles outside his cottage door, strumming the unplugged Rickenbacker, and didn't hear me arrive. I just stood and gazed at him. I'd thought I'd never see him again. I loved him so much it hurt. I wanted to laugh and cry and turn cartwheels all at the same time.

Carefully, I fish my sunglasses from under the cushions of the swing seat and cover my eyes. I'm going to cry again. Goodness — it has to be hormones or something! It's just that on this oh-so-reminiscent morning, I can still see Lewis as he was that day. Those tattered jeans, his silky hair, his eyes, his smile . . . I remember so vividly the happiness I felt at that moment, and the sadness that followed . . . No — I sniff quickly in case Mum and Dad notice — I mustn't think about it anymore. I really mustn't. In a very short time I must behave like a grown-up and go off to lunch with Mum and Dad, and of course I'll smile and laugh . . . The memories mustn't get in the way. Not today. I try to think about something else — but somehow, that very special moment insists on creeping in again . . .

'Hello . . . '

'Clemmie!' Considering the expense, he chucked the guitar down with unseemly haste, and jumped to his feet. 'Oh God — I've missed you so much!'

He pulled me close to him, and kissed me, and I knew it was going to be all right.

In between holding each other and kissing and just being, well, in love, we managed to catch up on everything that had happened. I was almost truthful about the exams, not so truthful about my parents, and absolutely truthful about Paula. It was a start.

Solstice, it appeared were going great guns, with bookings right up until the end of July. Lewis thought I should wear my school uniform for ever and ever and was most put out when I told him I intended to burn it. He was even more appalled when I told him I'd thought he was seeing Paula. We laughed a lot, talked a lot more, and kissed more than either.

'And now we've got the rest of forever to be together,' he said. 'Life couldn't be more beautiful.'

12

The next few weeks of that scorching summer were absolute bliss. I worked at Sheldon Busbys on Saturdays, and sometimes in the week, and picked fruit at Honeydew, too. My university fund grew in the post office; I'd bought some new clothes, as opposed to second-hand, and a pair of false eyelashes; my parents were happily planning a celebration party for when the exam results came out; Jenny and Dawn, primed by Paula, were pea-green about Lewis; my doubts about my A levels started to recede, and life was truly love and peace perfect.

Solstice were being booked all over the country, and I travelled to gigs with them in the transit whenever I could. As my parents still didn't know that Lewis existed, I used all sorts of mythical new friends from work to explain away my late nights, and no longer felt guilty. My guilt had all been linked to school and skipping my revision: now it was over and I was free. And one day Mum and Dad would meet Lewis and love him as much as I did, I was sure of that. It was just a matter of timing . . .

My most enduring memories of that time will always be sitting on Lewis's lap, as the van rocked and rolled into unfamiliar towns; watching proudly from the side of the stage as Solstice wowed another audience; listening to the radio playing songs like *Bad Moon Rising* or *Je T'Aime* in the darkness on the way home. We'd stop off at transport cafes in the early hours, sharing tables with weary long-distance lorry drivers, drinking strong coffee from thick white mugs and eating fried egg sandwiches, with the echoes of the night's performance ringing in our ears, laughing and planning our future.

Sometimes Gus, Vin and Berry brought their current girlfriends along too, but as they changed them as regularly as their socks, I never got to know any of them very well. Jez's long-term girlfriend, Hazel, occasionally came up from Bournemouth and we formed a sort of youthful dowager aunt outfit, becoming very sniffy about these transient groupies.

It was a wonderful, wonderful time to be young.

The first of July dawned, equally as scorching as flaming June had been. I was at Lewis's cottage. I'd been fruit picking all morning and improving my suntan in my cut-off jeans and a skimpy vest top. Lewis and Gus were working on a batch of new songs. The television was on: Lewis had a colour set and to me, as we only had black and white at home, it was like being at the cinema. We'd just watched the Investiture of Prince Charles, looking so young and dashingly handsome, by the Queen in the sunshine at Caernarfon Castle.

There was so much going on in 1969 ... Funny, I thought, that in a couple of generations time this would all be history and schoolchildren would be learning about it and finding it quaintly old-fashioned.

'We're just going up to the barn to run through these,' Lewis waved the sheaf of music scores at me and picked up the Rickenbacker. 'Are you coming with us? Or is your nose still stuck in that book?'

Lewis had bought me the new paperback version of Frenchman's Creek the previous weekend and I was really hooked on Dona's spirited love affair and adventures. 'I'll be over in a bit. I've nearly finished and I want to find out how it ends.'

'I knew it would happen. I knew you'd soon lose interest in me,' Lewis laughed and kissed me. 'See you later then — if you can tear yourself away.'

I threw a cushion at him, then stretched out on the sofa, with the doors and windows wide open to the drowsy heat and lost myself in the story.

'Noooo!' I reached the end, and hurled the book down in disgust. 'How could she bear to do that? How could she go back to that boring pompous prig? How could she leave her dashing pirate and — '

'Lewis?' A rather high-pitched voice coo-eed from the courtyard. 'Are you at home?'

I didn't even have time to scramble from the sofa before Mr and Mrs Hawton-Ledley, Jess and Henry, Lewis's Godparents, were inside the cottage.

'We've got a little surprise for you — oh!' Mrs Hawton-Ledley peered at me. 'Who the devil are you?'

'I didn't know Lewis had staff!' Mr Hawton-Ledley guffawed.

'Aren't you one of the village girls?' Mrs Hawton-Ledley asked. She pronounced it 'gels' and I wanted to laugh. 'What are you doing here? It's private property you know.'

'What's going on in here — oh, I say!' A very elegant middle-aged man in a sports shirt and flannels was laughing over Mrs Hawton-Ledley's shoulder. 'Hello, my dear. Are you a chum of my son's? I'm Jonty Coleman-Beck. Lewis's father.'

Completely panic-stricken at being in the company of a doctor — and a London brain surgeon at that — who just happened to also be Lewis's father, I made a sort of babbling noise. 'Er — hello . . . I'm Clemmie — um — Clementine Long.'

Mr Coleman-Beck laughed. 'Then Lewis has clearly inherited my impeccable taste. Lovely to meet you at last, Clemmie. He's told us so much about you — Lydia will be furious that she's missed you.'

Lydia, I guessed was Lewis's mother, and I thanked the Lord that she wasn't there too. It was like something out of Monty Python — of course they would be called Jonty and Lydia — my Mum and Dad were Frank and Jean.

Still stunned to think that Lewis's parents knew about me while mine knew nothing about him, I slid from the sofa. Very aware that I was far too skimpily dressed to be 'meeting the folks' for the first time, I muttered my hellos, shook hands all round, thought I really should curtsy, and sort of explained to the Hawton-Ledleys that Lewis and I were — um — friends, and that he was in the barn rehearsing some new songs and maybe they'd like to pop across and see him there.

Mr and Mrs Hawton-Ledley snorted down their aristocratic noses like two cart-horses and declined, but Jonty Coleman-Beck beamed with enthusiasm. He was so much like an older version of Lewis that I felt a bit more at ease. If I could just forget his elevated career status and his preposterously well-bred voice, I might even like him . . .

'Lead on then, my dear. I do want to see what that wastrel has done with all the money we've thrown at him. And if he doesn't turn into the next Mick Jagger after giving up Oxford then I'll disinherit him!'

Mr Coleman-Beck strode across the courtyard to the barn, with me trotting nervously alongside. I wished I could have forewarned Lewis — but I needn't have worried. The father and son reunion was joyous. I was impressed at the easygoing relationship Lewis clearly had with his father. And even more impressed with the pride in his voice when he introduced me.

'Far too late,' Jonty roared with laughter. 'We already know all about one another, don't we Clemmie? Not only did you not do her justice when you told us about her, but she's far too good for you, my boy. Your mother is going to adore her. But just in case you thought this visit was entirely social, there is something I need to discuss with you, so if you put down that overpriced banjo I'll treat you both to a rather late lunch or very early dinner.'

'Great, thanks, but now you're here you've got to hear what you've funded. Just tell me what you think of this . . . '

Lewis jumped back on to the stage, picked up the Rickenbacker, and Solstice thundered into one of Gus and

Lewis's new songs. It was foot-tapping, catchy, and very, very sexy. There were also, if you listened carefully, those few jaunty opening bars of *My Darling Clementine*, interspersed among the rock riffs. Blushing, I bit back a smile and stared at the dusty floor before sneaking a quick look at Jonty.

He was grinning hugely, clapping his hands and stamping his feet. When it was over he gave a long whistle of approval. 'Bravo! Encore! Splendid stuff! And all inspired by this young lady, I'll be bound! Not as classy as Matt Munro, of course, but pretty damn good. Now I must just have a word with the other long-haired layabouts . . .'

Jonty rushed over to chat animatedly with the rest of the group and Lewis and I exchanged conspiratorial grins across the barn. It was going to be okay and Jonty was, of course, wonderful if slightly exhausting in his exuberance. But meeting him only illustrated again the massive gulf between Lewis's upbringing and my own . . .

We eventually went off to eat in a new restaurant on the outskirts of Reading. I wore one of Lewis's soft denim shirts as a dress because there was no way on earth I could be seen in public in my shorts and vest. We roared away from Honeydew in Jonty's Jag — he had a Jag, naturally — and I wondered just how long it would take Mr and Mrs Hawton-Ledley to spread the word about me and Lewis round Ashcote.

Maybe it was high time that I introduced Lewis to Mum and Dad. And if I introduced them at the party *after* the exam results then there would be no recriminations, would there?

I voiced this over lunch. This was because I was far, far too nervous to eat. It was the first time I'd been into a proper restaurant for a meal. We simply didn't go out for meals. Mum and I sometimes had lunch in the Cadena when we shopped in Reading, but that was it. And as I was now faced with a plate of lobster thermidore ordered by Jonty, umpteen knives and forks, and two waiters hovering far too close, talking seemed preferable to eating.

I also thought that if I could see how Lewis tackled his lobster, then I'd know where to start. And I vowed to eat it even if I didn't like it. I liked fish — it couldn't be that different, could it? I just wished it didn't look quite so — well — whole . . .

'My parents are going to throw a little party when the A Level results come out in August,' I played with my bread roll. 'Well, not on their own of course, but with a few of the other parents — in the village hall.'

'That sounds like fun,' Lewis winked at me across the table, still not touching his lobster. 'And will you all be in your school uniforms?'

'Oh, definitely.'

'Then count me in. In fact, count Solstice in — we'll provide the entertainment.'

I was just about to say that would be just perfect when Jonty got to grips with the lobster's claws and a pair of nutcrackery things. I winced and pushed my plate away.

'Sorry to spoil your plans, then,' Jonty munched happily. 'But this was the reason for my visit. There's not much point in having friends in high places if you can't use them — and Eric, one of my old college chums, has a night-club or three in West Germany. Well, after the Beatles, British groups are all the rage over there and he's invested his money well — and he says if you're any good he'll give you a stint. Top of the bill. Excellent money.'

Lewis grinned. 'That sounds great — wow, Germany! A lot of bands got their big breaks out there. So when would it be? And how long for?'

'There's the rub,' Jonty demolished a second claw. 'He'd want you out there at the beginning of August for a three month residency.'

Three months! I couldn't be without

Lewis for three months!

Lewis shook his head. 'But that would mean not being back here until the end of October and Clemmie would be going up to Durham by the end of September and — '

Jonty laughed. 'Oh, the pangs of young love! Don't be so silly, you're far too young to give up everything — you've both got your entire futures ahead of you. You'll have to go your separate ways and meet up when you can . . . Absence makes the heart grow fonder and all that.' He munched happily through another few mouthfuls of lobster. 'Anyway, Lewis, have a chat to the other boys, but I'll need to know by the end of the week. Eric won't wait any longer than that — he'll book someone else in and you'll have lost your big chance. He's got a lot of friends in the recording industry too — they're always out there scouting round for fresh talent.'

I felt sick. Lewis *had* to go. I knew that. It was the break Solstice had been waiting for. But, oh, why now? We'd already talked about how we'd cope with being apart when I went to university — but that seemed ages away. We'd at least have the summer together . . . Now we'd only got a few weeks left, then he'd be in Germany and I'd be in Durham and it was nowhere near enough.

'Aren't either of you going to eat your lobsters?' Jonty raised his eyebrows. 'Too much in love to eat are we? Oh, I remember it well! Lydia and I used to pine dreadfully. Still, I hate to see food go to waste — shove 'em over here, then Clemmie.'

Once Jonty had demolished all the lobsters leaving a carnage of shells, and Lewis and I had picked at the salad and pushed a gooey trifle around our plates, we all whizzed back to Honeydew. And of course Solstice agreed to go to Germany. There was no other choice to make.

13

The pending trip to Germany put a real dampener on our otherwise blissful summer.

I worried myself sick that Lewis would meet someone else while he was away. I'd seen how the girls threw themselves at the band everywhere we went — the transit was now so covered with lipstick messages of love that you couldn't tell what colour it had once been — and Lewis was only human and far too good-looking, and — I tried to push it all out of my mind.

We simply had to make the most of the few weeks we had left.

'We're on a countdown,' Lewis said gloomily, 'like the Apollo mission.'

I sighed. Lewis might just as well be going to the moon. Without a phone I'd have to rely on letters and they'd probably take forever to arrive from

Germany. I knew I'd write every day — but what if Lewis didn't write back? What if he forgot all about me? What if . . . what if . . . what if . . .

I voiced these fears to Paula the following Saturday. She was the only person I could talk to properly. We were rushing round Reading in our Sheldon Busby lunch-hour, diving in and out of dark, noisy boutiques, trying on clothes in places like Biba and Chelsea Girl.

'It'll be horrible for you,' Paula said, posing in the entrance to the fitting room in a micro-mini dress of magenta psychedelic swirls, with a matching feather boa round her neck. 'But if you really, really love one another it'll be okay. I mean, you're not going to look at any other boy while you're at university, are you?'

I stopped in the middle of tipping a big floppy brimmed purple hat at different angles and looked at her indignantly. 'No, of course not!'

'Then why would Lewis look at other girls? Oh, come on Clemmie — he loves you, doesn't he?'

'So you say . . . '

'You mean he hasn't?' Paula flicked at the feather boa. 'He hasn't told you?'

'Not in words, no.'

She grinned. 'And have you told him?'

'Of course not! I know the rules!'

The boy had to say it first, of course. Everyone knew that.

'Tell him, Clem. I know it's only words, and we both know how he feels about you — but if you *say* it it'll make all the difference.'

'What if he doesn't though? I'll feel so stupid.'

'But he will because he does,' Paula insisted. 'And he probably feels just the same as you do. He's probably scared to say it as well. Now — what do you think of this? Shall I buy it? Will Nick like it?'

Paula and Nick Rayner were still together. Wearing thigh-high boots and the shortest skirts in the world, she roared through the village on the back of his motor bike making all the parents

— mine included — tut-tut their disapproval.

'Nick'll love it. Paula, can I ask you something else?'

'Uh-huh,' she nodded as she struggled back into her skinny sweater, careful not to dislodge her false eyelashes.

'Are you on the pill?'

Her glossy dark head popped out of the neck of her jumper like a jack-in-the-box. 'Course I am! Do you think I'm stupid? Why, aren't you?'

I put the floppy purple hat carefully back on its stand. 'Oh, yes . . . Yes, of course I am. I'm not stupid either.'

Which is why I made the appointment to see Dr Dawson as soon as possible.

Two days later I scuttled into the waiting room of Ashcote Surgery, avoiding everyone's eyes, sure that they'd know why I was there. They were all friendly with Mum and Dad and had known me since I was born. Fortunately they were too busy swapping stories about their ailments and

146

commenting on the weather and the space race and all the village gossip, to have noticed me.

'You looking forward to university, Clemmie?' Mrs Turner, the receptionist shouted, poking her head over the desk and immediately drawing me to the attention of the entire waiting room. 'Your mum and dad are as proud as punch.'

I nodded noncommittally and hoped everyone would go back to talking about the minutiae of Ashcote life. Of course they didn't. They all stared at me.

'You got that summer bug, young Clem?'

'She'll be in for her jabs before she goes off to university.'

'Maybe it's women's trouble. She's at that funny age.'

I was never more delighted than when Dr Dawson's imperious voice crackled my name over the intercom. I shot into her surgery and sat down, staring at my feet.

'And what seems to be the trouble?'

I looked up at her. She was about a hundred years old and had treated me all my life. I was absolutely terrified of her and squirmed with embarrassment. I seemed to have had to do an awful lot of growing up in a very few weeks. It was ironic that when I first met Lewis I hadn't even kissed anyone and now I was here, taking this huge adult step.

I swallowed. 'Er — well . . . that is . . . ' I couldn't do this. Yes I could. I took a deep breath, knowing I was blushing scarlet. 'Um — I want to go on the pill.'

Dr Dawson peered at me over the top of her glasses. 'And is this because you intend to behave promiscuously at university?'

'No, of course not!'

'So you have a fiancé here in the village do you? I don't remember your parents telling me you were getting married.'

'I don't . . . I'm not.'

Dr Dawson sat back in her chair. 'Clementine, the contraceptive pill is not to make it easy for young girls like you to throw their morals out of the window, you know. It's for married couples to be able to regulate the size of their families. I don't approve of the moral decline in this country and will not condone it professionally. You are far too young.'

'I'm seventeen and a half. And I'm — I mean, it's 1969 — and the pill — '

'Is available to be prescribed at my discretion. And I will only prescribe it for married couples.' She leaned forward. 'The best advice I can give you, Clementine, is simply to say no until you are married.'

I thought about Paula. 'But other people are on it — '

'So they might be, but unless they're married they wouldn't have been prescribed it by me. I'm not prepared to add to the morass of iniquity among the youth of this country. I'm sorry.'

I slunk out of the surgery feeling grubby and embarrassed. The Swinging Sixties were clearly never going to reach the darker corners of Ashcote. I knew I'd have to ask Paula how she'd got the pill, and where — then realised that I couldn't because she already thought that I *had*.

And of course by the time I got home everyone in the waiting room had told my Mum I was there and I had to endure the Spanish Inquisition all over again. Inventing a sudden bout of hay fever, I sneezed a lot and took to wearing sunglasses all the time and felt even more guilty than I had before.

And there was still the love thing to get out of the way . . .

14

One night, in the middle of July, we were travelling home from a particularly hectic gig, and the night was like deep black velvet, the way it is in high summer just before the dawn. Gus, Berry and Vin were asleep on the seat behind us, and I was curled on Lewis's lap, trying to hold on to the moment, trying not to think how desperately lonely I was going to be without him.

Jez leaned over from the steering wheel and turned on Radio Luxembourg. *I'm Going To Make You Love Me* wafted out into the warm dark silence. I snuggled against Lewis and sang the words under my breath.

'It's too late,' he spoke softly in my ear. 'You don't have to try.'

I stopped singing. I almost stopped breathing. 'Sorry? I mean — '

'I already love you, Clemmie. I love

you so much it hurts. You'll never have to try to make me love you.'

I could have cried with happiness. 'I love you, too.'

'Thank heavens for that,' Jez laughed. 'Mind you, I never thought there was any doubt myself.'

I hugged myself with glee. It was going to be all right. Just as Paula had said it would be. Lewis loved me. And because he loved me we'd survive the imminent parting and our later separations and nothing, nothing in the world would spoil it.

On July 20th, I stayed up all night in the cottage with the rest of Solstice, and I had my first ever taste of champagne as, with open-mouthed amazement, we watched Neil Armstrong and Buzz Aldrin emerge from Apollo 11 and walk on the moon. It was one of those spine-tingling 'do you remember what you were doing when?' moments. I knew that one day I'd bore my grandchildren rigid with stories of sharing this history-making event with a beautiful, way-out-of-my-social-sphere, love-of-my-life, bohemian musician who I'd never, ever forget even when I was very, very old.

The moon landing also seemed to sum up the era. Things were changing, everything was exciting and forward looking. Nothing was impossible. Everyone could achieve whatever they wanted: it was a year for dreams to come true, mine included.

The last days of July arrived far too quickly. All too soon I knew that Lewis would be leaving for Germany, and our time together would be at an end. I'd decided to wait until after he'd left for Germany and then tell Mum and Dad about him. That would give them a few months to get used to the idea before they actually met him, during which time there'd be all the excitement of me leaving Ashcote and starting college; and of course I knew I'd have to confess all — well, some — of my untruths, but they'd understand, I knew they would.

Saying goodbye to Lewis was one of the most painful things I've ever done. Solstice were to fly out from the latest recently-opened terminal at London Airport, and much as I wanted to spend every last second with Lewis, I knew that a trip to London and then having to find my way home while completely heartbroken, was out of the question.

Which was why we said our goodbyes at Honeydew on a shimmering golden morning. All the equipment and musical instruments had been crated and carefully packed and had left the day before. Vin, Berry and Gus could hardly contain themselves. Jez was quiet and sad, having spent two days in Bournemouth with Hazel, and Lewis and I were simply desolate.

Of course he wanted to go; it was his career after all. I knew how torn he was, and there was no way I'd make it more difficult for him. Eric, the night-club owner in Germany, had even arranged for a taxi to collect Solstice from Honeydew and take them to the airport. The driver sat, drumming his fingers on the steering wheel, as Lewis and I clung together. It was just like *Leaving On A Jet Plane* . . .

'Why do you have to be going to Durham?' Lewis muttered into my hair. 'Why couldn't you have gone to university somewhere nearer? Durham's the other end of the country!'

I sniffed. I knew that. And Germany might as well be on the other side of the world.

'You'll write as soon as you get there, won't you?' I mumbled.

'I'll write when I'm on the plane and every day after that,' Lewis tipped my chin up. 'I hate to see you cry . . . And you'll let me know your address in Durham won't you? And — oh, God, Clemmie . . . '

'Much as I'm reluctant to break up you lovebirds,' the taxi driver laughed, 'I've been instructed to get you to the airport by midday and you'll miss the flight if we hang about any longer.'

We kissed goodbye then.

'I love you,' Lewis whispered. 'And I need you and I want you and I'll see you really soon.'

'Half term . . . ' I didn't even try to stop the tears. 'I'll be here at half-term. I love you so much.'

I stood and watched through a blur as the taxi rattled out of the courtyard, spitting up clouds of dust, and waved until it was out of sight. Then in the scorching heat which had suddenly turned icy cold, I walked away from the cottage and the courtyard and Honeydew, and my world seemed dark and empty.

For the next week or so Mum and Dad, still planning the celebration party and not knowing why I was so miserable or why I spent a lot of time playing *Make It Easy On Yourself*, discussed it all with Jenny and Dawn's parents. I heard them all huffing over the difficulties of having teenage daughters with their emotional upheavals. It was like living on a roller-coaster, they said, which was exactly how I felt.

As the days went by, Paula, Jenny and Dawn helped a lot, of course, and I still had Sheldon Busbys to keep me busy. I worked practically full-time because I simply couldn't face fruit picking at Honeydew. I'd never felt so awful. I couldn't eat, felt sick, slept badly, and for no reason at all, cried over the most ridiculous things. Roller-coaster summed it up perfectly.

Lewis, true to his word, wrote straight away and told me about the club and the flat which Eric had found for them, and about Germany — but mostly about how much he loved and missed me. Mum and Dad assumed I now had a German pen-pal and I didn't disabuse them of this notion. I wrote long airmail letters by return, telling him every tiny detail of my life, and taking them to be weighed and posted at the Ashcote Stores became the highlight of my day.

I missed him more and more. I didn't get used to being without him: on the contrary, the gap in my life grew wider, the ache in my heart seemed to grow more painful each day. I wondered how on earth couples had coped in the war when they'd been torn apart never knowing when, or even if, they'd see each other again.

And then came the day that changed everything for ever: Thursday August 19th 1969. Two letters arrived for me, neither of them from Lewis. The first contained my A level results. The second confirmed that I was pregnant.

15

'What time is it, Clemmie?' Mum calls across the garden. 'Should we be getting ready?'

Her voice makes me jump. The memories are so vivid that for a moment I'm completely disorientated. Gathering my scattered wits, playing for time, I slowly take off my sunglasses, fold the Sunday papers and look at my watch. It's new. Beautiful. My parents' present to me. 'Er — oh, almost eleven. The restaurant's booked for twelve thirty and we're going to walk, so it depends how long it's going to take you to get glammed up.'

'Hours,' Dad laughs. 'She's as bad as you, Clem. You might both be ready by teatime.'

'Excuse me,' I look at him indignantly. 'I'm ready. I've been ready for ages. It doesn't take me long to put my face on these days. Less is more when we women reach a certain age.'

Dad winks at me. 'Not like it was when you were a youngster, eh? All those thick black lines and false eyelashes! You used to look like Dusty Springfield!'

They both stand up, smiling, and head for the house.

Dusty Springfield . . . Lewis always said he loved my Dusty Springfield eyes . . .

I try really hard to think about now. About today. About my new outfit — slim black trousers and a pale blue silk shirt — classic and unfussy, although I still prefer to wear jeans . . . No, I mustn't look back. I must concentrate on today. On the impending lunch at Cookery Nook, Ashcote's newest and trendiest restaurant. It's very difficult. After so much reminiscing, the past is still very, very real.

On the day that those two earth-shattering envelopes arrived I'd fled out here into my parents' garden, crouched under the cherry trees, and opened them with cold, shaking hands. I'd been swamped with a terrified, stomach-churning foreboding. I'd looked at the letters and the words had danced before my eyes. If the result of the pregnancy test had confirmed my worst fears, the A level results simply compounded them.

A in English . . . C in Art . . . D in RE . . .

Nowhere near good enough to get into Durham. Not that it mattered. I wouldn't be going to university. I wouldn't be going anywhere ever. Sometime, just before my 18th birthday, I'd be a mother.

Feeling sick, giddy, terrified, I clumsily stuffed the envelopes into the back pocket of my jeans and hurried out of the garden. I had to find Jenny and Dawn before they came whooping round to the house, and Mum and Dad discovered the awful truth.

I met them at the bottom of the lane,

and knew from their ear-to-ear smiles that they'd achieved exactly the grades they'd needed. Trying not to cry, not to feel eaten up with envy, I muttered that, apart from English, mine hadn't been very good at all and that I'd tell Mum and Dad later and would appreciate them keeping out of the way.

They looked at me with sympathy and said it didn't really matter, that Durham would probably take me anyway on the strength of my English grade and my interviews. Which might very well have been true if it hadn't been for the fact that I was pregnant.

In a complete daze I caught the bus into Reading, and stared out of the window at the scorched, parched countryside seeing none of it. What on earth was I going to do?

I couldn't tell Lewis. I simply couldn't. Not now. Not yet. Maybe not ever. He'd leave me of course. He was far too young to want to be tied down with a baby. He'd probably deny it was his. I had to face this alone.

Oh, but Mum and Dad! How ever would I tell them? They'd go completely crazy. They'd be so angry, so disgusted, so ashamed of me. And so hurt. And disappointed. I'd let them down in the worst way possible. They'd never get over this. I whimpered and brushed the tears away from my cheeks. My life was in ruins — and it was all my fault.

Sheldon Busbys was hot and packed. *Honky Tonk Women* was blaring from the speakers.

'Hello, Clemmie,' Mr Smithson yelled. 'Come in to give us a hand, have you? We could do with it!'

I shook my head. 'I — um — just wondered if I could see Paula, please?'

'She's on her break. Upstairs.'

The tea room at the top of Sheldon Busbys was built into the roof space, and the sky was pure blue through the skylights and the sun beat down in shafts of molten gold. I shivered. Paula was drinking coffee and eating a doughnut at a corner table. My stomach lurched and I suddenly felt very sick.

'Hiya,' Paula waved the doughnut. 'I didn't think you were in today.'

'I'm not,' I sat opposite her, trying not to look at the doughnut or smell the coffee. 'I needed to talk to someone . . . to you . . . oh, Paula . . . '

'There-there.' She patted my heaving shoulders. 'It can't be that bad, Clem. Nothing's that bad.'

'This is,' I gulped. And told her.

When I'd finished she said nothing. Her eyes were wide with shock and sympathy. Leaning across the table she called to one of the other girls who was just finishing her break. 'Linda, tell Mr Smithson I won't be down straight away, will you? Tell him I'll work through my lunch hour. Ta.'

She looked at me. 'What a mess, Clem! What are you going to do?'

'I don't know.'

'But how — I mean — you're on the pill.'

I shook my head. 'I'm not. I wasn't. I

lied. And Dr Dawson wouldn't prescribe it . . . but it was too late by then anyway . . . '

'And Lewis?'

'I told him I was on it,' I looked down at the orange plastic-topped table. 'It seemed easier. I wanted him to think I was grown-up and sophisticated.'

'Oh, Clemmie!'

'The baby's due in March so even if Dr Dawson had said yes it would have been too late and — '

Paula exhaled. I blessed her for not telling me again how stupid I'd been. I already knew. I'd been doubly stupid — messing up my A Levels and getting pregnant — just because I'd fallen once-and-forever in love with the most beautiful boy in the world.

'So you won't be able to go to university? Blimey! Your Mum and Dad will go mad!'

'I know. I know. Oh — what am I going to do?'

We looked at one another. We both knew that despite the enlightened

Swinging Sixties, girls who 'got into trouble' really had few options. There had been plenty of girls in Ashcote who had been in my position and they'd either disappeared to stay with distant relatives, or were booked into one of the far-flung mother and baby homes, having the baby adopted, and returning to the village alone looking pale and distraught and with their reputation in tatters.

'Look, you've got to tell your Mum and Dad. It'll be awful, I know — I wouldn't fancy it — but they've got to know. And you should tell Lewis — '

'No!' I shook my head. 'I don't want him to know!'

Paula frowned. 'Why on earth not? He loves you, and it's half his problem after all. If it was me I know Nick would be — '

'Nick and Lewis are totally different. You and Nick have known each other for ages, and Nick will work at the garage in Ashcote for ever and ever. Lewis is rich and from another world.

We've not known each other very long. He's just starting out on his career — and his parents will kill him if he fouls up on this as well as on Oxford. He won't want to know.'

'Tough,' Paula shrugged. 'It takes two to make a baby.'

'But only one to be pregnant. It's my fault. All mine. And I'll deal with it alone. no-one needs to know about it apart from you — and Mum and Dad, of course.'

We stared at one another again. I knew I had to tell Mum and Dad. I'd tell them about the exam results first, and then about the baby. I knew exactly how they'd react. I knew exactly what they'd say. It was the last thing in the world I wanted to do . . .

16

It was far worse than I could ever have imagined.

The tears, the pain, the accusations, the recriminations: I'd simply broken their hearts.

They were as angry and as shocked as I'd known they would be. They treated me as I deserved to be treated. I'd been a cheap silly little fool. That about summed it up. I apologised over and over again but Mum and Dad were too distraught to listen. They hurled all the late nights, the absences, the lies — oh, so many lies — at me. I haltingly told them the truth, far too late, but I confessed everything except Lewis's identity.

They couldn't even begin to believe the magnitude of my deceit. As I listened to myself, I wondered why I'd ever felt it necessary to tell so many untruths. Then came all the things I'd known there'd be: the 'what will the neighbours think?' and the 'after all we've done for you' and the 'how could you let us down like this'. In their anger, they called me some awful names. But worst of all was their genuine heartbreak that my university career and my entire future was ruined. That I'd ruined it myself in such a cavalier fashion.

They also assumed that the baby was Nick's and that it was because of my friendship with Paula that it had happened at all. They both came in for some unfairly harsh words. Of course I rigorously denied this. When I wouldn't tell them who the father was, they then assumed that I didn't know and were even more angry. I said nothing. White-faced, they blamed themselves, me, everyone else, then me again.

The next few days were terrible. Now I knew I'd lost Lewis for good my heart was really breaking. I was horrified at what had happened to me. Frightened to death. And I was distraught at what I'd done to my parents. How could I have been so stupid?

We barely spoke. The atmosphere at home was appalling.

'You'll have it adopted,' Mum said about three days later, viciously preparing a salad in the kitchen while I sat at the table. It wasn't a question. 'And I suppose you could retake your A Levels and see if Durham will want you next year.'

Dad had just come home from work, and nodded. 'It might be a way out of it, I suppose.'

I swallowed. 'I'm not having the baby adopted.'

They both stared at me as if I was completely mad.

I shook my head. 'I'm not going into one of those homes and I'm keeping the baby. And if that means that I have to leave here, then I will. If you don't want anything to do with me or your grandchild . . . '

'Grandchild?' Mum blinked at me.

'Don't try that on us, Clemmie. This isn't our grandchild, for heaven's sake! Grandchildren come along a decent interval *after* the wedding in this family! Don't be so silly — you can't keep it!'

'I can and I am. And it is, you know. Your grandchild. Part of me. Part of you.'

And part of Lewis, but I didn't say so. And the reason why I'd never give up my baby. It would be the only tangible part of him I'd have left.

I let them digest this in silence. It would break my heart to leave home, to have my baby alone, to try to manage as best I could, to bring it up without help — but I'd do it. I knew I would.

I stood up. 'I'm going upstairs. I don't want any tea. When you've decided whether I can stay here or not to have the baby, I'll come back down again and find out.'

I flew into my bedroom and slammed the door. *Make It Easy On Yourself* drowned the sound of my tears.

17

'Clemmie! Visitors!' Dad appears in the kitchen doorway. 'And very pretty they are too!'

I scramble to my feet from the hammock swing, grinning. Dawn and Jenny rush down the garden path towards me and we all giggle and shriek excitedly as if we were children.

We've never lost touch, and always celebrate high days and holidays together. Jenny has been married and divorced twice, has a son from each marriage, and teaches RE at an independent school on the outskirts of London. Dawn married a boy she met at university, is still happily in love, has three children, is a very proud and brand-new grandmother and works for a bank in the Midlands.

We admire one another, pretty sure that we've aged well and glamorously, and all talk at the same time, catching up on the gossip. Whenever we meet we're still the same three girls who grew-up together, went to school together, played together. Still friends. We never quite set the world on fire as we'd intended, but we've all been lucky with our lives.

'I can't wait for this lunch,' Jenny says, patting her flat size 10 stomach. 'I'm starving and I've heard good reports of this new restaurant. Who else is going to be there?'

'The usual crowd . . . including Paula and Nick, of course,' I say, laughing.

Jenny and Dawn laugh too. Nick Rayner, the undesirable heartthrob of Ashcote, is now the owner of the Ashcote Garage, and quite a little gold mine it is, too. Nick is now plump and balding and is becoming an elder statesman of the village. No-one would believe he was a black leather tearaway in his youth. He and Paula married in the early-seventies and are still in love. They have four children, all of whom married young and have children of their own, all of whom still live in Ashcote. They are a huge and happy family. Paula, now the village post-mistress, is round and mumsy and a million light-years away from the flirty nymphet of our teenage years.

'Anyone else?' Dawn asks. 'Any nice men for Jenny?'

I shake my head. 'I'm not introducing Jenny to husband number three — I'm sure she'll find him without my help. Anyway, there'll be —'

We're interrupted by Louisa, my daughter, waving from the back door. Louisa. My only child. She's 33 now. I still can't believe it. She's tall and slim and so beautiful. Heartbreakingly beautiful. Just like her father.

'Mum! Cookery Nook are on the phone!' Louisa runs down the path, waving her mobile. 'They're ready for us.'

'Fine,' I smile. 'And are Granny and Granddad ready to go?'

Lou and my parents adore one

another. They always have done. From the minute she was born.

She nods and grins. 'And Granny's wearing a really bad hat.'

We exchange mock-horrified glances. Mum still likes to wear a hat for special occasions. Neither Lou nor I would be unkind enough to dissuade her from her notions.

In the usual last minute hoo-hah over making sure the door is locked, and that everyone has handbags and hankies and that the cars aren't blocking the lane, I watch Louisa fuss round Mum and Dad. She's a lovely girl — woman, I mean. We're very close. And she's just become engaged to Ben who she works with in an Oxford book shop. I'm pleased. I like him enormously. He'll be waiting at Cookery Nook with the rest of the party.

Lou did everything I should have done: three excellent A Level results followed by university, although not Durham, a career in book-selling which had been her ambition since she'd first learned to read, and, before Ben, plenty of boyfriends.

Boyfriends . . . Lou's had lots of boyfriends — but none of them, as far as I could judge, generating the white-hot passion and deep once-in-a-lifetime love that I'd shared with Lewis. Not even Ben. Lou and Ben are blissfully happy, and sure of their commitment to one another, but they've never seemed to have that heady, giddy, pulse-thundering relationship that I'd had.

Now I'm walking along Ashcote's sleepy lanes again with my family and dearest friends towards Cookery Nook which has been built on the site of the old infants school where Mum was a cleaner. Everyone is talking non-stop. The sun spirals from a clear September sky and the verges are still head high with waving grasses and wild flowers. Nothing much has changed in Ashcote.

Once Mum and Dad had realised that I was serious about keeping my baby, they did what everyone had said they would, and helped me far more than I deserved. For a while I'm sure they thought I'd change my mind and have it adopted, but until then they put on brave faces around the village, and made sure that if people made cruel remarks about my condition then they never reached my ears. Paula, too, was a tower of strength in those early months, always there for me, always on hand to listen. Even Mr Smithson in Sheldon Busbys came up trumps. He said he saw no reason why I shouldn't continue to work for as long as I was able.

Which, of course, left Lewis . . .

As everyone with any inkling of pop music will know, Solstice became one of the best-known and top-selling groups of the late 60s and early 70s — only going into decline with the arrival of the punk era.

Lewis's dream came true even if mine had bitten the dust in truly spectacular fashion. I smile again at the memories as I walk along, my arms linked through Jenny and Dawn's

— just as we had on our journeys to school a lifetime before.

Remembered scents of dog roses and columbine and the sweet rich perfume of privet flowers hangs languorously on the air. Time slips away once more as I'm drawn back to the past . . .

18

The autumn of 1969 was as glorious as the summer had been. Mum and Dad, although still not happy about my pregnancy, were beginning to accept its inevitability. They still knew nothing about Lewis, and when his letters arrived from Germany I read them and stored them unanswered in my dressing table drawer. Because I knew how Lewis would react, I decided simply not to tell him.

I just stopped writing to him . . . no, that's not true. I still wrote to him every day — long letters pouring out my heart and my love — but I never sent them, except for one brief one to say goodbye. It was for the best. There was no point in prolonging the agony.

His letters to me became more and more anxious. He simply couldn't believe that I'd stopped writing. That I didn't want him any more. Neither could I. But it was the only way . . .

Towards the end of October, when Solstice were due back from Germany, I was nearly five months pregnant. I was working full-time in Sheldon Busby's and had discussed Lewis's return with Paula over and over again.

'He knows where you live,' she said. 'He's bound to come round and see you. He'll want to know what's going on.'

I shook my head. 'He thinks I'm at university by now, doesn't he? Anyway, I wrote and told him it was over and that I'd met someone else.' It was the only letter I'd posted.

Paula's jaw dropped. '*What?* What on earth for?'

'So that he can get on with his life and so that he doesn't have to finish with me and so that he doesn't feel obliged to — '

'He loves you and you love him!' Paula almost stamped her foot, making Mr Smithson frown along the counter.

'You are so stupid!'

'I know.'

What other choice did I have? For the next couple of weeks I hurled myself into my work, even though everything about Sheldon Busbys reminded me of Lewis. Again all the songs were poignant — none more so than the heartrending *Nobody's Child*. Paula always turned it right down every time someone wanted to hear it. I still cried, though. Everything made me cry. How long ago it all seemed when life was just lovely, and I was playing at being Marianne Faithfull and never once considered the consequences.

'Clemmie, there's a problem with booth 4,' Mr Smithson said. 'Are you up to checking the speakers? Someone wants to listen to *Everybody's Talkin'* and apparently can't hear it. You can manage it, can't you my dear?'

I nodded. Mr Smithson wanted to wrap me in cotton wool. He was lovely to me. I'd tried to explain that I was pregnant, not ill, and being young and healthy had never felt better. At least, not physically. But Mr Smithson seemed to think I should be at home with my feet up and not lift a finger.

I tapped on the door of Booth 4 and walked in.

'Hello,' Lewis stood up from one of the stools and pushed the door shut behind me. 'Now would you like to tell me what exactly is going on?'

I stared at him. Oh, how I loved him! How I'd missed him! This was like a dream come true. I had to force myself to stand still and not hurl myself into his arms.

Trying to stop myself from shaking, I took a deep breath. 'I gather you don't want to listen to Nilsson, then?'

'No. What I want to know is why you stopped writing, why you're not at university, why you've dumped me for someone else, why — ?'

I blinked back the tears. 'Did Paula — ?'

He shrugged. His face was stony. 'Paula came up to Honeydew, yes. She told me not to take any notice of the only letter you managed to send, and that you wanted to talk to me but that I mustn't, under any circumstances, go to your house. So I didn't, and here I am and I really think I'm owed some sort of explanation, don't you?'

I rubbed at my eyes, knowing my mascara would smudge and that I'd look like a panda. It didn't matter. I simply stared at him. I'd missed him so much and I'd love him for ever but I had to let him go.

'You know how it is . . . '

'No I don't!' Lewis grabbed my shoulders. 'I love you, Clemmie. I hated every minute of being in Germany even though it's probably made our career and we've got a recording contract and a tour and all sorts of stuff out of it. All I thought about was you. I missed you every second of every day and night. All I wanted was to come home and be with you. I thought you felt the same! What happened to change you? Us?'

'This . . . ' I lifted my long T-shirt.

My stomach swelled slightly under my denim skirt.

Lewis stared down at it, then at me. And his eyes filled with tears.

19

But the past is over. Gone. Alive only in my memories and my dreams.

We've reached Cookery Nook. There are balloons and a banner outside and I laugh.

'Go on Mum,' Louisa pushes me forward. 'You first . . . '

I walk inside. It's quite dark, with little twinkling wall lights and candles and silver sequins scattered on the pristine white table cloths. There are roses everywhere. And then from the darkness, there's music.

A rollicking version of 'Oh My Darling Clementine' bounces from the walls.

Solstice, older, but still drop dead gorgeous, are playing on the little dais above the tiny woodblock dance floor. Lewis, tall, slim and devastating and still looking like Scott Walker crossed with David Bowie, grins at me. I grin back through the tears. I adore him.

The rest of the party pouring into Cookery Nook joins in on the chorus. I blush and am very relieved when the waiting staff emerge with the champagne buckets and their notepads. Everyone is finding seats and chatting across the tables.

I'm delighted to see Ben catch hold of Louisa and cover her face with kisses. Jonty and Lydia Coleman-Beck are with Jess and Henry Hawton-Ledley and are greeting my parents like the old friends that they are. Mum adjusts her hat to a jaunty angle. Dad laughs.

'I still fancy the drummer,' Jenny whispers as she and Dawn find their seats with Paula and Nick. 'Is he currently available?'

'Vin has just divorced wife number four,' I whisper back. 'He's even ahead of you in the multi-marriage game. You'll make a lovely couple.'

Lewis has unplugged the Rickenbacker and crosses the floor.

'Congratulations . . . ' he pulls me towards him and kisses me.

'We've already done that this morning,' I kiss him back. 'But thank you — and for all this. This is even better than I'd ever dreamed.'

'I promised you this,' he whispers into my hair. 'And I always keep my promises, don't I?'

I nod, fighting back the tears and kiss him again.

'Dad!' Louisa calls across the restaurant. 'Put Mum down! You two are *so* embarrassing sometimes! Come over here and tell Ben about your new tour. He thinks you're really cool.'

Lewis laughs as he does as he's told, and I laugh as well. Solstice have recently been asked to take part in a 'Celebrate the Sixties' UK tour with other bands from the era. It's been a source of massive amusement in the family, with dire warnings of men of a certain age being far too frail for the temptation of sex and drugs and rock'n'roll, and that they'll be better off with multivitamins, a milky drink and Terry Wogan.

I slide into my seat and gaze around the restaurant. Everyone I love is here, under one roof. Mr Smithson, long retired, and his wife are with the girls I worked with all those decades ago. There are old school friends, and Solstice and their wives, and our new friends made over the years, and our families all mingling together. Everyone is eating, drinking, talking and laughing.

No-one deserves to be this happy.

Lewis and I still live at Honeydew. We moved into his cottage immediately after our 1969 Christmas wedding. It snowed, and over my pregnancy bump I wore a white velvet dress with a swansdown hood like Lulu had when she married Maurice Gibb. Jenny, Dawn and Paula were bridesmaids in matching crimson velvet mini-dresses. We had the reception at Honeydew and honeymooned in Jersey. Lewis and I were deliriously happy then — and we still are.

Of course, now the four labourers' cottages have been knocked together giving us a spacious home. And we own Sheldon Busbys. Lewis bought it when their first LP, 'Solstice — Summer and Winter', went platinum. So yes, I've worked in Sheldon Busbys all my life on and off. It's still as it was, with the listening booths, and the original layout and vinyl records: a shrine to the music of earlier decades, and as you probably know people come from all over the world just to say they've been there.

Jonty and Lydia have been wonderful parents-in-law, and Mum and Dad love Lewis almost as much as I do. Life has been very kind to us and we do appreciate it. I have no regrets at all.

'Happy?' Lewis takes my hand as the tables are cleared and coffee is served. My silver bangles jangle, the newest one, his present to me this morning, shining slightly more brightly than the others which I've worn all my life.

'Blissfully. As always.'

'Shall I make the announcement, then?'

I pull a face. 'Yes, I suppose so — but please, please make it brief — I'm so embarrassed.'

He kisses me slowly and with love. 'You should be proud. I am. You've achieved something that I didn't have the gumption to do . . . I love you so much . . . '

I watch him as he walks across to the raised dais. I know I'm blushing.

'Thank you all for being here today to celebrate with Clemmie,' his deep husky voice rings out from the microphone. 'It's made a very special day even more special . . . I know you'll all join me in a toast. I'm so very proud of her — my beautiful wife, my gorgeous best friend — ' he pauses and laughs, 'so please raise your glasses and drink a toast to my very, very clever darling Clementine!'

I know I'm going to cry again. My cheeks are scarlet as everyone raises their glasses and echoes the toast. They are as proud of me as Lewis is.

You see, at the vast age of fifty one, I

have just achieved the last of my ambitions and gained a first class honours degree in English. At last, I've been to university — oh, not Durham of course, I was a mature day student at Reading — and amazingly passed with flying colours.

We'd attended the official ceremony earlier in the year of course, when Lewis and Lou and Mum and Dad had been bursting with pride as I'd tottered on to the college stage in my gown and mortar board to collect my certificate — but this, today, with all my friends, is even more precious.

Lewis holds up his hands for silence. 'There's one more thing to do before we get down to some serious celebrating . . .'

The rest of Solstice join him. I notice with amusement that Jenny and Vin have to stop holding hands. Hazel, Jez's wife, beams at me from across the restaurant. She knows.

Solstice take their place on the dais again and Gus is waving the microphone.

'As you all know, we're shortly going

to relive our ill-spent youth by hitting the road again. We're intending to reprise our repertoire of those first heady days of the Swinging Sixties and as we've got a captive audience we thought you'd have to suffer our first practice run . . . '

Everyone claps and laughs.

The lights dim and much to everyone's amusement Solstice run through a few riffs of *My Darling Clementine*. Then Lewis moves forward . . .

'This is from me to Clemmie. With all the love in the world for ever, darling. As it was then, it is now, and will be for our eternity..'

Then he starts to sing . . .

Make It Easy On Yourself . . .

I shiver as the frisson tingles my spine and our eyes meet in absolute love. My happiness is complete. Now and forever.

We do hope that you have enjoyed reading this large print book.

Did you know that all of our titles are available for purchase?

We publish a wide range of high quality large print books including:
Romances, Mysteries, Classics
General Fiction
Non Fiction and Westerns

Special interest titles available in large print are:
The Little Oxford Dictionary
Music Book, Song Book
Hymn Book, Service Book

Also available from us courtesy of Oxford University Press:
Young Readers' Dictionary
(large print edition)
Young Readers' Thesaurus
(large print edition)

For further information or a free brochure, please contact us at:
Ulverscroft Large Print Books Ltd.,
The Green, Bradgate Road, Anstey,
Leicester, LE7 7FU, England.
Tel: (00 44) 0116 236 4325
Fax: (00 44) 0116 234 0205